"Do you know anything about babies?"

At Toby's query, Marcus looked absolutely horrified. "Babies?" he asked. "Why should I know anything about babies?"

She replied ruefully, "Well, most men your age are married with families. I just thought you might."

"Well I don't. Neither am I married." And he made it sound as though being married were on a par with having some infectious disease.

"Well, don't you have any other family who could look after your nephew?"

"Definitely not."

Then, as he turned toward her with a gleam in his eyes, Toby backed away. "Oh, no. Not me. I barely know one end of a baby from another."

"Well, that doesn't surprise me," he said squashingly. "I have yet to find anything you can do except drive me insane."

EMMA RICHMOND

take away the pride

Harlequin Books

TORONTO • NEW YORK • LONDON
AMSTERDAM • PARIS • SYDNEY • HAMBURG
STOCKHOLM • ATHENS • TOKYO • MILAN

Harlequin Presents first edition September 1989
ISBN 0-373-11203-3

Original hardcover edition published in 1988
by Mills & Boon Limited

CHAPTER ONE

'YOU didn't give them to me!' Toby exclaimed in exasperation, and she just wished he wouldn't look at her with that pained expression, as though she was deliberately trying to persecute him. She wasn't. In fact, she was trying very hard to be efficient, and it was most unfair of him not to at least try and appreciate that fact.

'Look,' he began wearily, 'I do realise you can't be expected to know where everything is—I'm not a complete fool—but I did ask, if you remember, that you don't file anything until you understand the system.'

'But I didn't,' Toby began, finding it extraordinarily difficult to concentrate when faced with piercing blue eyes that seemed to make her brain into more of a mush than usual. 'You truly didn't give them to me.'

'Yes, I did.' And the blue, blue eyes that Toby found so fascinating hardened, developing a definite glint that Toby was beginning to discover usually presaged a burst of temper.

Taking a deep breath and holding it for a moment, he finally managed, really quite calmly, 'Just before lunch, I asked if you'd finished typing the report.' And Toby nodded solemnly, she did clearly remember that. 'I then handed you two sheets of paper and asked you to attach them to it—didn't I?'

Screwing her face up into a comical little grimace, she shook her head apologetically. 'No. You had some papers in front of you, and perhaps you meant to give them to me,' she said kindly, 'but you didn't. Mr Dawson rang through and you told me to go to lunch, which I did. Maybe you put them in your briefcase,' she addded helpfully.

'I did not put them in my briefcase,' he gritted between his teeth, 'I gave them to you. Go and look.'

Knowing the sheer futility of doing any such thing, Toby nevertheless got to her feet and went back to her office.

'And, Miss Anderson,' Marcus said softly, from so close behind her that she jumped in alarm, 'while you are looking, perhaps you would keep an eye open for the files that disappeared yesterday.' And, before Toby could think of a suitable retort, he'd gone again. Grinding her teeth in fury, she threw herself into her chair in an attitude of exhaustion. How on earth, she wondered, could she ever in a million years have thought herself capable of working for the autocratic Marcus du Mann? However had she thought those bright blue eyes might gleam with laughter? The wretched man had no sense of humour whatsoever! 'And I didn't file anything!' she yelled aloud in an effort to relieve her feelings. 'And you didn't need to make that crack about losing your precious papers, either!' She bet they were in his briefcase. Did she dare go and look? No, she decided, she didn't; with her luck he'd come back and catch her.

Getting up, she went to the cupboard and removed the brown manila folder that contained all the papers Marcus had given her during the week she had been working for him, which she hadn't filed, she mentally reiterated. Swiftly riffling through them without any expectation of finding the papers he wanted because she knew very well he hadn't given them to her, she closed it with a snap. Walking to the filing cabinets, she solemnly went through each drawer. No files. It wasn't that she was stupid—far from it, she just wasn't a dedicated secretary type. Balance sheets and reports and typing long, detailed letters on cost analysis and justifications bored her silly. Leaning her elbows on the top of the cabinet and resting her chin on top, she stared through the window. Blue sky, fluffy white clouds, the solitary tree that was all she could see from her office, that was where she wanted to be, outside in the fresh air. Well, maybe not fresh, she qualified with a little grin, not in South London, anyway, but at least she wouldn't get this feeling of claustrophobia. Half closing her eyes she conjured up sparkling waters, people shouting and laughing lithe bodies cleaving the waves, a warm sun . . .

'Praying for divine intervention, Miss Anderson?'

Swinging round in shock, her too hasty movement making her bang her elbow on the edge of the cabinet, Toby stared at Marcus for a moment, her lovely amber eyes blank. She kept forgetting how tall he was, and every time he stood before her she felt as though she were shrinking. She'd never considered herself particularly short, yet beside him she felt

like a midget, and to actually stare up into his face
made her neck ache. He was also impossibly beautiful, the sort of man who made your knees go weak.
Not because you wanted him or fancied him; it was
like looking at a beautiful painting, it brought a
funny little flutter to the throat, a little bump to the
heart, made you sigh at its sheer perfection.
Absently rubbing her arm she shook her head, which
caused an errant strand of pale toffee-coloured hair
to escape the confinement of her precarious topknot.
'No, sorry,' she said lamely, irritably trying to poke
it back in. 'I was just debating whether or not I had
the nerve to go and rummage in your briefcase.'

'And what was your conclusion?' he asked softly,
with a wry lift of one eyebrow.

'That I didn't,' she admitted.

'Very wise. However, just to prove that I'm not
the ogre you seem to think, *I* will go and look.'

Following him into his office, Toby admired the
broad back clad in its expensive suit jacket, not a
wrinkle to mar its perfection; but then, a wrinkle
probably wouldn't dare appear, she thought with a
grin. Immaculate, that was the word for him. It
would be hard to imagine him unshaven, scruffy.
Even casual. His shirts were always crisp, his suits
pressed to within an inch of their life, and the tall,
straight body never lounged. He didn't lean against
walls as other lesser mortals, neither, so far, had he
removed his jacket, despite the heatwave they were
currently enjoying. Everything about him was
precise: his speech, his actions, his mind. The thick
dark hair just touched the collar, and she found herself clenching her fingers tight to stop herself doing

anything so silly as putting a hand to touch it to see if it felt as silky as it looked. 'Cracking up, Toby,' she murmured to herself, then gave a lame smile as he turned in surprise.

'Sorry?' he queried.

'Nothing,' she mumbled. 'Just talking to myself '

As he snapped open the catch of his briefcase, she surreptitiously crossed her fingers, an action that didn't go unnoticed by Marcus, she saw. Peering over his arm, she watched him rifle swiftly through the papers and then stop. Peeping sideways at him, she watched his lower lip thrust forward in a gesture of self-disgust before his eyes swivelled towards her.

'My apologies, Miss Anderson.' he said quietly.

'Accepted, Mr du Mann,' Toby said solemnly. 'We all make mistakes,' Then she gave a soft little laugh and wagged her finger at him. 'You don't need to add that I make more than most.'

'No,' he murmured blandly and Toby could have kicked herself for putting words in his mouth. 'Perhaps you would now kindly attach them to the report,' he said, passing the papers to her.

'Certainly—and no, I have not lost the report,' she said, forestalling him.

Leaning his hips back against the desk and folding his arms across his chest, he asked sardonically, 'Not by any chance Irish, are you?'

'Irish?' she asked in astonishment. 'No, or not as far as I know. Why?'

'Oh, no reason,' he said dismissively, then, straightening, walked behind his desk. 'When you've attached those, bring your book through, would you? I've a letter that needs to go tonight.'

Quickly doing as he asked, she sent up a swift prayer to a hopefully benign deity that this time she'd be able to read it back.

'It's to Don Anderson at Hi-Tech,' he said as soon as she was seated. 'You'll find the address in the book. If I go too fast, stop me,' he said firmly, giving her a stern look. 'We don't want a repeat of yesterday's fiasco, do we?'

'No,' Toby mumbled, although it was odds on that it would be. She'd told him at the interview that her shorthand was rusty, but the truth of the matter was that it was practically non-existent; she had never finished the evening-class course that she had taken in both typing and shorthand, and anything that required hooks or short forms were quite beyond her capabilities. Only she didn't think he would be very amused if she asked him to only use words of one syllable. She couldn't even use the excuse that he mumbled or didn't speak clearly, because he did. He didn't speak loudly, but he had a clear, precise voice. Neither did he stumble over what he wanted to say; he spoke with fluency and intelligence, the sharp brain behind that rugged face always ahead of his vocal chords. Not like some people.

'All right?' he queried.

'Yes,' Toby mumbled, hastily ironing out her frown. Only please don't ask me to read it back, she prayed.

'OK, that will do,' he dismissed. 'Jackie can take it with the rest of the post.'

Desperately trying to hold the phrases in her

head, and altering her notes as she walked, she went back to her office. Propping her notebook on the typewritter, she pressed the sensor to put her work into memory. That was one advantage of the new word processors, she could alter away to her heart's content until she got it right. Or hopefully right. Unfortunately, Marcus always remembered exactly what he'd said and, while he would probably be prepared to accept one or two variations, the decimation of whole text would drive him into a fury, and Toby wasn't sure she had the energy to cope with another of his tempers. Not today, at any rate. Whoever would have thought being a secretary was so exhausting?

When she thought she had it right, or as right as she was ever likely to get it, she printed it out then took it through for his signature. 'Thanks,' he said absently, his dark, well-marked brows pulled into a frown of concentration which became even more pronounced as he read the letter. Toby's heart sank. Tossing it down in front of him, he leaned back in his chair, an expression of disgust marring his rather aristocratic face. 'About the only thing right with it is the address. If you couldn't do shorthand, why the hell say you could? All you've done is waste both my time and your own.'

Tempted to tell him it was his own fault for not giving her a test at the interview, one look at his face disabused her of that little notion. 'Well?' he barked.

'Sorry,' she mumbled guiltily.

'And that makes it all right, I suppose?'

'No.' But she could hardly explain because that

would no doubt drive him into an even greater fury.

'Oh, for God's sake!' he said wearily, throwing his pen down on the desk in disgust. Then, taking a deep breath to contain his temper, he continued more reasonably, 'Look, Miss Anderson, I have a great many important things to do in my day and I need a secretary to carry the load. Not only to check my appointments, make sure I have the correct papers for meetings, but to be able to lay her hands on anything I might need at a moment's notice. Now, I don't expect all this to happen in the first week of you joining us, but I get the feeling you don't give a damn about whether I'm satisfied or not.'

'I do!' she exclaimed, rather horrified that he thought otherwise. She knew she wasn't the world's most efficient secretary, but she had been trying. 'I am trying,' she insisted, 'but everything is so unfamiliar—the jargon, the technicalities. I've been going through the files to try and memorise all that's going on, but there seems so much.'

'Then ask the receptionist! I told you she would help out at first. I realise you've been dropped in at the deep end, but you don't seem to be thinking! I need someone to know my needs before I know them—I simply do not have time for the day-to-day running of the office!'

'I know that! And I'm sorry that I'm not being more helpful—but you're not the easiest man to work for, you know! You make me nervous . . .'

'I do what?' he exclaimed, astonished.

'Make me nervous—and when I'm nervous I panic. It's not that I can't do things, it's that you don't give me time to get my thoughts together . . .'

'I don't have time to pander to you!' he burst out incredulously.

'I didn't ask you to!' Toby snapped crossly. 'But there's no need to treat me as though I'm four years old and backward!'

'Oh, good grief,' he muttered, staring at her as though she were a species he'd never come across before. 'I told you how it would be at the interview, and you seem quite confident that you could cope.'

Then she'd been a better actress than she'd thought. 'I can cope.' she murmured helplessly,' but you have to give me time. I'm not supergirl, you know!'

'That's patently obvious.' he muttered.

'Well, there's no need to be sarcastic—and if you don't tell me what you want, how the hell am I supposed to learn? You don't explain properly, you just say this or that without explaining just exactly what this or that is! I'm not telepathic!'

'You're not anything at the moment except a damned nuisance,' he said irritably, then, as though even he thought that was a bit harsh, added, 'All right, I admit I'm impatient--and there is absolutely no need to cast your eyes up to heaven in that fashion,' he put in shortly. 'If you are going to list shortcomings, your list on present performance is going to be a hell of a lot longer than mine!'

And ain't that the truth, she thought guiltily, her anger with him subsiding.

'Well, isn't it?'

'Yes,' Toby muttered. 'But I don't do everything wrong! You make me sound an absolute dilly!'

'I didn't say you did. You answer the phone very nicely.'

'Oh, thank you!' Toby retorted sarcastically. 'It's a wonder you managed to think of any plusses at all!'

'Well, it was difficult,' he murmured, his mouth twitching, involuntarily she was sure. 'But,' he continued, his face becoming serious again. 'If you want to continue working as my secretary, you'll have to make a bigger effort than you have to date.' Then, with the rapid change of subject that was so characteristic of him and which always seemed to leave Toby half a dozen paces behind, he said, 'It's too late to do this letter now, the last post will have gone—we'll do it in the morning. But I would strongly advise you to buy yourself a shorthand instruction book—your version of Pitman doesn't seem to bear much to the original at all!'

Giving a little snort, Toby turned and walked back into her office, sorely tempted to tell him what he could to with his job, only she couldn't afford grand gestures. 'And you can stop looking so smug!' she muttered crossly as she came face to face with the receptionist.

'Do you always talk to him like that?' she asked, her fine fair brows raised. 'Not very subservient, are you?'

'Subservient?' Toby spluttered. 'Why the hell should I be subservient? Damned autocrat! What do you want, anyway?' she demanded. She'd taken a complete and utter dislike to the tall, blonde receptionist, not only because of her refusal to help Toby out, despite Marcus's injunction that she do so, but because of her sneering attitude to Toby

herself. She might not be the world's most efficient
secretary, but there was absolutely no need for Nina
to make disparaging remarks. That was just unkind,
and if there was one thing that drove Toby into a
fury, it was people being unkind.

'I merely came to collect the letter Mr du Mann
said was to go tonight.'

'Well, you can't! I haven't done it yet.' Toby
hastily held the letter behind her back. But even
someone with limited eyesight couldn't have failed
to notice the slashing blue pen lines that Marcus had
made through it, and the receptionist certainly
didn't have that. Miss Perfection personified, Toby
thought waspishly.

As Nina swung away with a taunting smile, Toby
glanced at her watch. Five-thirty. Did anyone ever
get away on time? she wondered drearily. Nine to
five were the designated hours, and so far this week
she'd not been away before six. Had it been a job
she enjoyed or could at least cope with, she knew the
extra hours wouldn't have mattered, but, as it was
each day seemed quite long enough without adding
another hour on top. She hadn't bound the board
papers either, but she really didn't think she could
face struggling with the wretched binding machine
again. She'd come in early and do them in the
morning. Hiding all the papers in the cupboard and
locking it, she collected her bag. Any feelings of guilt
were now overshadowed by Marcus's quite
unnecessarily scathing comments on her ability. Or
lack of it. One could only take so much in one day.

Brooding on the day's events as she walked home,
because she'd given her bus fare to a little old lady

collecting for the local hospice, Toby wondered if it wouldn't be wiser all round to admit defeat now before she became a nervous wreck—or Marcus did.

'You're late,' her flatmate exclaimed as Toby pushed open her front door.

'Mmm,' she murmured absently. 'I walked.'

'And?' Sally enquired with a laugh. 'No, don't tell me, someone conned you out of your bus fare.'

'No, they didn't . . . Oh, well,' she murmured deprecatingly, 'she looked in more need of it than I did, and it was a nice day for a walk.'

'Oh, Toby, you're hopeless. Is it any wonder you're always so hard up? Any old sob story and you'd give your last penny! Apart from that,' she grinned, 'what sort of day have you had today?'

'Don't ask,' she groaned. 'I tell you, Sally, that man is driving me insane! He doesn't know how close he came today to being stabbed with the telex spike!' Pushing through into the lounge, she threw herself on to the sagging old sofa in an attitude of defeat. 'Do you know what he asked me today?' she demanded. 'Do you? And, as Sally shook her dark head helplessly, 'He asked me if I was Irish! Now why on earth would he ask that?' she questioned, looking totally perplexed. 'Do I look Irish?'

Her brown eyes sparkling with amusement, Sally perched on the arm of the chair opposite, querying, 'However did I come to think you were stand-offish or lacking in humour? Your tales of the hapless Marcus each evening are better than a play!'

'Hapless?' Toby demanded. 'He's not hapless, he's an infuriating maniac!'

'And do you suppose he goes home to his wife

or family each evening to regale them with tales of
you?' she asked, tongue-in-cheek.

Looking slightly startled for a moment, Toby
suddenly grinned, the sense of humour that was
usually such an integral part of her returning, then
gave a warm, rich, infectious laugh. 'Do you know,
I never thought of that,' she murmured, a little
gleam of mischief in her eyes; but, if she did give him
sleepless nights, it was no more than he deserved.

'I'd love to be a fly on the wall at his house,' Sally
observed rather wickedly. 'Oh, boy would I just love
that. Did you find the files you lost yesterday?'

'I didn't lose them!' Toby exploded. 'He never
gave them to me! Honestly, Sally, I spend hours
scrabbling in those damned filing cabinets like a
demented squirrel, and we both know I'm not going
to find anything. He hides things in that blasted
briefcase of his and pretends he's given them to me!'
Shaking her head ruefully, she hauled herself to her
feet. 'I'm starving, whose turn is it to cook?'

'Yours,' Sally said drily.

Pulling a face, Toby sauntered into the tiny
kitchen where she peered hopefully into the
cupboard and fridge. 'Eggs on toast?' she asked.

'What, again? I shall look like an egg soon. OK
OK,' she agreed, holding her hands up in
surrender. 'Eggs on toast will be fine. But I really do
feel that one of us ought to take a cookery course,
otherwise we'll either both end up with malnutrition
or an egg-bound disease, and although being thin
has its advantages, if I want to break into model-
ling, an egg-bound disease definitely does

not!'

When they had eaten and were both nursing their coffees at the rickety kitchen table that neither could afford to replace, Toby mused quietly, 'I bet his last secretary didn't leave to get married at all. He probably murdered her and buried her body in the grounds.'

'If anyone is going to end up buried in the grounds, it will be you, my girl. I hate to say this, Toby, but you don't seem entirely suited to this job, and it seems very doubtful if you'll even last out the months's trial.'

'Yes, that's what he said,' Toby murmured, giving Sally a humorous look.

'Well, if you dislike him so much, why work for him at all? It seems crazy to me.'

'I don't dislike him. Not exactly,' she murmured evasively. 'I want to, but there's something rather endearing about someone who's always so grumpy.' She smiled softly as Sally gave a shout of laughter. 'Well, there is,' she insisted, and it was true, she didn't totally dislike him. Well, not all the time.

'So now tell me the real reason,' Sally demanded quietly after a rather pregnant pause. 'Come on, you never did tell me how you got the job, or why you're working as a secretary when you hate secretarial work, and especially working for a man you don't like and can't cope with?'

'Oh, I can cope with him,' Toby said confidently, 'if I'm allowed to stay around long enough to do so.' Then, giving her friend a wry look from beneath her lashes, she murmured, 'There was this advert in *The Times*—and the money was so exceptional that I . . .'

'Ah!' Sally exclaimed, beginning to understand. 'The rent.'

'Well, I can't keep sponging off you!' Toby exclaimed, embarrassed.

'You aren't. I told you that. Oh, Toby, why do you have to be so damned proud? I told you we can manage until you find exactly what you want.'

'No, you can't! And if you could, you shouldn't have to! We're supposed to be equal partners in this flat, share and share alike—and all I've done for the past two months is sponge off you!'

'And if the positions were reversed? Would you throw me out?' Sally asked drily. 'No, of course you wouldn't, you'd do exactly as I'm doing. Give it up, Toby. Something will turn up.'

'Yeah? When?' she asked despondently. 'When I'm too old to teach,' she muttered. 'I can just see me, old and wrinkly in a saggy knitted swimsuit, teaching children to swim from the side of the bath because I'm too old and feeble to get in the water.'

'Oh, Toby, don't be ridiculous!'

'It isn't ridiculous! There just aren't any vacancies for swimming instructors!'

'Well, what about the parks commission? They said they'd have some vacancies soon.'

'They've changed their policy, they're taking students instead—they don't have to pay them so much. And this job is good money, Sally,' she added determinedly. 'And paid weekly while I'm on trial.'

'But you hate it.'

'No, I don't. Not hate, exactly. It's just that I seem to get claustrophobic shut up in an office, and when he shouts at me I get in a panic and lose things.

I expect I'll lose the board papers or something tomorrow,' she added gloomily, picturing Marcus's fury if she did so.

'You never get in a panic,' Sally observed, laughing, 'or at least you haven't in the the six months I've known you. You're the most easy-going person I've ever met.'

'Not when he's around, I'm not.' Then, flicking Sally a wide-eyed glance of pure devilment, she grinned. 'He has trouble finding anything about me to recommend, and I hardly think easy-going is a qualification he would come to admire.'

'Didn't anyone else apply?' Sally asked curiously. 'Fate isn't usually so co-operative finding a well-paid job just when you need it.'

'Ah,' Toby murmured wryly, 'I was the only one with the right qualifications.'

'A swimming teacher?' Sally exclaimed, astounded. 'How on earth does that qualification make you desirable as a secretary?'

'Mm, well, I have some more now,' she added, an infectious grin tugging at her mouth. 'I made some up.'

'Oh, Toby, you didn't!'

'Oh, Sally, I did.'

'What?'

'Oh, a few O-levels, a few As,' Toby said airily.

'How many?' Sally demanded, giving Toby a look of severe reproof.

'Eight O, four A—bit over the top, would you say?' she asked with a gurgle of laughter at Sally's shocked expression.

'But how on earth can you get away with fictitious

qualifications?' Sally asked, astounded. 'Didn't he check?'

'No, like you. I expect it never occurred to him that anyone would make up qualifications they didn't have.' And in view of Sally's shock, she'd better not tell her she wasn't very good at shorthand, either.

'You'll forget what you've said.'

'No, I won't,' Toby said triumphantly. 'I kept a copy of my CV.'

'You'll lose it,' Sally prophesied.

'No, I won't.'

'Yes, you will. You lose everything. And what happens if he finds out? He doesn't sound at all the sort of man to be amused.'

'No-o, I don't think he'll be amused,' Toby confirmed. 'I expect he'll sack me. Anyway, I don't suppose the situation will ever arise,' she said with marvellous confidence. 'He's already told me that if I don't pull my socks up, he'll get rid of me. I think, to be honest, I'd better start looking round for something else. Only it's so well paid, Sally! But I can see I'm hardly his perfect soulmate,' she intoned, her sorrowful glance belied by the twinkle in her eyes.

'What does he imagine this perfect soulmate to be like?' Sally asked, not quite sure whether she should be amused or horrified.

'Oh, I don't know, someone svelte and sophisticated like you, I suppose,' she explained without rancour, and with a deliberate attempt to get off the subject of her qualifications, or lack of them. Smiling, she continued, 'No matter how hard I try, svelte and sophisticated is not how I come out.'

'Oh, I don't know,' Sally murmured, tilting her

head on one side, 'You have beautiful hair, the colour of which a lot of women spend a fortune trying to achieve. You have a nice figure, full bust, narrow waist.' Pursing her lips thoughtfully, she finally pronounced, 'But I have to admit, Toby, that fond of you as I am, the whole does not add up to outstanding sophistication. You have the dearest face, but . . .'

'At six, Sally, a dear little face is fine, not to say an asset,' Toby said drily, more amused than anything else by her friend's obvious desire to find something complimentary to say, 'but at twenty-four, a dear face is not quite what I would like to aim for. That's the whole trouble, everything I have adds up to "nice". "Nice" is so lame, Sally! I mean, what turns it into "exciting"? "Terrific"?'

'You have a sexy voice. If those low, husky tones send a shiver down my spine, what do they do for men?'

'I don't think my voice does anything. Not that I've noticed, anyway. On the phone, yes, but who wants to be thought sexy down a phone-line? When they meet me face to face I'm hard put not to giggle at the looks of astonishment I receive. It's very discommoding.'

'I don't think there is such a word,' Sally laughed. 'And I seem to remember Brian found you sexy,' mentioning the man who had lived beneath them when Toby first arrived. He had moved about two months ago, presumably to find someone more accomodating than either herself or Sally.

'No, he didn't,' Toby snorted. 'He thought I was easy game. Anyway, I don't want to be sexy, I want to be svelte!' she added, hastily skating over that particular incident before Sally could probe further. It wasn't something of which she was particularly proud. She had rather liked Brian until she had found out he was unemployed. No way was she ever going to allow herself to be put in the same position as her mother. When her father had had his accident and been unable to work, being self-employed and with no insurance, he hadn't got paid, and she could still very clearly remember living hand to mouth. If she ever fell in love, she was determined it would be someone not necessarily wealthy, but certainly in good employment. It was rather a cynical attitude and certainly not very laudable, but she didn't think she would have the same sort of courage as her mother. Those years of struggle before her father died, of his increasing bitterness at being a cripple, were burned indelibly into her brain, and not even to Sally could she explain the years of first anger, then self-pity, that her father had gone through. All the years he had been working, healthy, he had been fine, good-humoured and strong. Sadly, he just didn't have the inner resources to cope as a cripple. The sympathy and kindness originally given to him had gradually disappeared. Visitors stopped coming and, although it was an awful thing to think, it had perhaps been a blessing in disguise when he'd developed a kidney infection and died just before her eighteenth birthday. She had loved him dearly, so had her mother, but those last years of his life had been a travesty. Being a cripple didn't only mean you sat in a wheelchair or lay in bed; if you were paralysed from the waist down, as her father had been, then it involved other aspects as well. Aspects that never occurred to the fit and healthy.

There was also the touch of guilt that she had never been able to earn enough to keep them totally free of debt. At sixteen, with no qualifications, it hadn't been very easy to find a well-paid job. A filing clerk in a local insurance company had been the best she could find, and she had been forced to go to evening classes three nights a week to learn shorthand and typing, which she had hated. Not that her parents had ever said, but she knew they, too, had felt guilty at allowing her to leave school without taking any exams. She had been quite bright and her headmistress had been furious, she remembered, but pride had prevented her from telling the head the reason. Looking back, it seemed ridiculous that she had been so proud and silly. The headmistress would surely have helped, tried to find a solution, if she'd asked.

'However did I manage before you came to share the flat?' Sally murmured, breaking into Toby's reverie. 'My life must have been incredibly dull.'

Forcing a smile, Toby teased, 'Peaceful, at any rate.'

'Mm, unlike poor Marcus's,' Sally said wryly, 'Still, if he didn't check you out . . .'

'No, and I bet that's the first time in his live he's ever taken a chance,' she mumbled, exchanging a rueful little glance with her friend. 'They were all at sixes and sevens, his previous secretary had already left, someone else was on holiday, and—well, he just took my word for it,' she added lamely. 'A godsend,' he'd said. She bet he wouldn't say that now, more

like divine retribution, and she began to feel a bit
ashamed of her impulsive behaviour. As she was
beginning to discover, being a secretary was a great
deal different from just a copy typist who could do a
bit of shorthand. It wasn't a question of being bright
or clever, it was a question of experience, and that
she just didn't have. 'Do you think me very awful?'

'Oh, Toby,' Sally said helplessly, 'how could I
think you awful? You're the kindest person I know,
and I do understand why you did it, not wanting to
get into debt and everything after your wretched
childhood . . .'

'It wasn't wretched,' Toby defended quickly. 'Or
not until Dad had his accident. It's just that I can't
bear to owe money—and now that I have some sort
of security, I'm afraid of losing it.'

'Well, I don't think you're going to find much of
it with Marcus du Mann,' Sally murmured, patting
Toby's hand in a comforting little gesture. 'What
does he look like?' she asked as she got to her feet to
replenish the coffee-cups.

'Very Celtic. Dark brown hair, bright blue eyes
that look as though they ought to twinkle, and don't.
Or not very often, I'd guess. Perhaps he had a
horrendous childhood,' she murmured, looking
suddenly thoughtful.

'Toby, Toby, don't for God's sake start
fantasising about saving him from himself. I know
you, you'll turn him into a project.'

'Nonsense, I just want to knock some of that
smugness out of him, that God-like air of
complacency.'

'Well, I wish you well, but I don't think I'd have

the nerve to make up qualifications.'

'Yes, well, I don't say I like lying, because I don't. But there wasn't any choice. I must have some money to pay the rent—and the gas bill,' she added, remembering that that was about due. 'And if I can just get through this month's trial,' she murmured, 'I should be all right for the rent at least, and then maybe something else will turn up. I'd never taken the flat on if I'd known that the job at the sports complex was likely to fold. I was so sure it would be permanent. That's what comes of counting your chickens,' she muttered gloomily.

'Now, Toby, be fair! You could hardly be expected to know that the wretched council were going to cut back on leisure activities. You weren't the only one to be made redundant, were you?'

'No—the football coach got his marching orders, too,' she smiled. 'Not that that makes it any easier to bear. Oh, well . . .' Giving a funny little shrug, she got quickly to her feet, exclaiming, 'Now, if I can get that crabby water heater to work, I'm going to have a bath and wash my hair. I have to be early tomorrow.'

'Dare I ask why?'

'I haven't made up the folders for the board meeting yet. They have this wonderful heat sealing machine which I haven't quite mastered.' And giving Sally a wry grin, she went to wrestle with the water heater.

CHAPTER TWO

SOAKING in the bath, Toby pondered Sally's words. Despite her flippancy, she wasn't unaware of the risk she was taking. Neither was she as insouciant as she pretended. Deception of any kind was anathema to her, and telling herself that she would have got her qualifications if she had been able to stay on at school was no justification for lying. Although her typing *was* accurate, she hadn't lied about that, even if it wasn't very fast, but that was only because she hadn't had much practice. Temporary work as a copy typist in between working as a swimming instructor didn't exactly make for proficiency. But Sally was right about Marcus's reaction should he ever find out, she thought, sighing. He wasn't going to take very kindly to the fact that he had been taken for a fool. Giving a long deep sigh, Toby debated whether to confess to him—only that would hardly solve the problem of the rent. Despite Sally's words, it might be months before she found a job she was actually qualified for, and the sports council hadn't been very optimistic. Openings for swimming instructors were very few and far between. Another problem was Marcus himself; it would be a great deal easier if she could actually dislike him, only she couldn't. Despite his rather autocratic behaviour, she found herself wanting to make excuses for his rudeness, and that was just plain ridiculous. Marcus du Mann didn't need anyone to make excuses for him, least for all herself. He was also quite devastatingly attractive, which was another problem she must overcome. Becoming attracted to him would be the height of stupidity. Apart for which, the Marcus du Manns of this world weren't for little girls like herself. Sally, maybe, with her high cheekbones and long legs, but not a gamine little five-foot-five nobody with funny-coloured eyes.

As she walked into the office at eight-thirty the next morning, the first person she met was Frank Dawson, the financial director. Giving her a beaming smile that made him look more than ever like a wizened monkey, he asked, 'Is this an attempt to ingratiate yourself with our lord and master, or simply because you didn't finish the board papers last night?'

'The latter,' she admitted wryly, 'and if you delay me in the corridor, I won't finish them now, either.' Then, grinning over her shoulder at him as she began walking away, she said, 'He adores me really, you know. He just pretends he finds me useless to throw people off the scent.' And she poked her tongue out at Frank as he gave a shout of laughter.

'Well, we're in good shape apart from the folders, and it won't take you long to finish those, will it?'

Laughing at his optimism, and glad that someone was in good shape, she walked the last few yards to her own office. As she pushed open the door she came face to face with Marcus on his way out. He looked even more austere than usual and Toby

wondered guiltily if he'd overhead her words to Mr
Dawson. She hoped not, although it was hard to
envisage his estimation of her going down any
further than it was already. Backing up a pace as he
did the same, so that they performed a complicated
little shuffle, he muttered impatiently, 'Oh, for
God's sake!' And, wrenching the door out of her
hand, he held it wide so that she could walk through.

'Were you looking for me?' she asked mildly,
moving across to her desk to pick up the pile of post.

'No, Miss Anderson,' he said shortly, his tone
leaving her in no doubt, had she ever harboured
any, that she was the last person on earth he would
ever look for. 'I was looking for the board folders.'

'They won't be long,' she answered with a
confidence she was far from feeling. 'I only have to
finish photocopying the pages and then bind them.'

'Well, bring them through as soon as you've
finished. Jackie can make my coffee.'

You could make it yourself, Toby felt like
retorting. She imagined Mr Dawson's secretary had
quite enough to do without pandering to him. Not
that Jackie would probably mind, she seemed to
view Marcus with a slavish devotion that Toby
highly amusing. As he left, she quickly rifled
through the post; then, deciding there was nothing
urgent, she collected the papers to be copied before
walking swiftly along to the general office, the speed
of her movements making the cream and brown
dress swirl seductively round her knees.

Running off eight copies of the board papers,
Toby quickly checked the front sheet agenda to
make sure they were all in the right order then with

a great deal of mental finger-crossing she switched on the binding machine. Putting each set of papers into the outer folder, checking that all pages sat neatly on the glued spine, she put them into the slot provided that would heat the glue and hopefully attach all the pages. In theory, it was simple, in practice, as she had discovered before, the pages took a malicious delight in falling out as soon as the folder was opened. Walking back to her office, the eight folders held carefully in her hands, she took them into Marcus.

'Don't open them!' she warned, hastily slapping her hand flat on top of the folder to prevent him doing so.

'How the hell are we supposed to discuss them if we can't open them?' he asked irascibly.

'I meant at this particular moment, not never!' Honestly, the man was impossible! He of all people should know that; he'd presumably been given board folders before. Taking a deep, much needed breath, she explained reasonably, 'The glue isn't dry. If you open it now, all the pages will fall out. You have to be patient.'

'Patient? Patient?' Marcus exclaimed incredulously, his well-marked brows almost disappearing into his hair. 'I've been waiting for these damned folders for the last hour! The board meeting is in precisely ten minutes,' he said shortly, shooting back his cuff to glance at his watch. 'Is everyone here?'

'All except Sir David.'

'Well, put them in the boardroom and make sure they have coffee.'

'I already did. I have also laid it up with pads and pencils, cigarettes, iced water and glasses. I'll bring in fresh coffee at eleven. Do you want a bar set up?'

'No,' he said bluntly. 'We'll break sharp at one. Perhaps you would kindly ensure that lunch is ready for that time.' The temptation to be sarcastic presumably got the better of him, as he added, 'May I have the rest of the papers?'

Staring at him, her eyes searched the deep, piercing blue of his in a futile effort to discover what papers he was talking about. Then she grimaced slightly as he sighed, long and deeply.

'The papers I asked you for last night. The papers I need for the meeting.'

'You didn't ask me for any papers . . .' she began slowly, frantically racking her brain for even the vaguest memory of him doing so. As far as she recalled, all he'd done was make caustic comments about her shorthand.

'Miss Anderson,' he gritted, his jaw rigid, a white line running along the tanned skin, 'I asked you for the financial report on Harpers,' he gave a nasty little smile as her eyes widened in recollection, 'and the draft contract for Hi-Tech.'

'Ah!'

'Yes, Miss Anderson—ah. Perhaps you would kindly fetch them. Now.'

Walking slowly back to her office, Toby leaned against the communicating door. Staring blankly at the row of filing cabinets, she tried frantically to remember where she might have put both items when he had given them to her on Friday. She remembered him giving them to her, she also quite clearly remembered him saying not to lose them, which was why she hadn't put them in the folder. Oh, hell! But what had he had not said was that he wanted them for the boarding meeting. Then, her mouth curving in a wide smile, she walked quickly over to her desk. Yanking open the bottom drawer, she retrieved the papers. The bottom drawer, she remembered, was where she had decided she should keep not-to-be-lost documents. Only she had temporarily forgotten that fact. Taking them quickly into his office, she had them practically snatched out of her hand. Tutting at his rudeness, she then smiled disarmingly as he gave her a look of fury.

Going back into her own office, she dealt with the post before having a much needed cup of coffee. She'd go and see the cook about lunch in a moment. When she'd answered what letters she could and put the others into Marcus's folder for action, she went along to the kitchen to make sure that the arrangements for lunch were in order. If the lunch were late, that would be the next drama. Fortunately her predecessor had left comprehensive lists of what to do on board meetings days, so it was a fairly simply matter to cope. It was the wretched paperwork that almost defeated her. Just before eleven, she tidied her wayward hair, tucking the errant wisps back into her topknot before going to make the coffee. When she had taken it into the boardroom, without actually spilling any or throwing it over the board members—much to Marcus's surprise, she guessed, judging by his expression—she returned to her office, then wasted several minutes while she tried to work out what it was about Marcus that set him apart from other men. He was the youngest member of the board, yet his comparative youth in no way diminished his aura of power. She'd noted that when she'd gone into the board room. He'd looked totally in command. Even Sir David seemed to defer to his obviously superior judgement . . . she jumped guiltily as the phone rang.

'Mr du Mann's office.' she said crisply, then blinked in astonishment as a woman obviously not far short of hysterics, demanded to speak to Marcus. 'I'm sorry,' Toby apologised, 'he's in a meeting at the moment. Can I help?'

'It's his sister, Wanda,' the woman said, sounding as if she were now crying. 'I need to speak to him desperately, it's very urgent.'

'Well, can you tell me?' Toby asked gently. 'Then if it's a real emergency, it might be quicker for me to explain to him.' She didn't dare interrupt the board meeting; he'd strangle her. By the time she'd managed to sort out the rather garbled story that Wanda unfolded in between bouts of crying—that her husband had had an accident somewhere in Malta where he was working, that she needed to go out there to be with him and that she had no one to leave her baby with—Toby was already busy with the flight schedule. 'Has Marcus got your telephone number?' she asked. It was no good assuming anything, because if he didn't she was the one who would get the blame. 'Right, now, I'll tell him and he will either ring you straight back or come down. All right? Meanwhile I'll see if I can book you on a flight and find out the details. Who does he work for? O.K.

I've got that!' Hastily scribbling all the information, Toby promised to get back to her as soon as possible.

Deciding it might be as well to get everything sorted out before telling Marcus, half hoping that the board meeting might have finished by that time, she first rang Wanda's husbands's personnel office at his company, Dent & Co., then the Malta High Commission. She had found in the past that embassies were usually very helpful, and this time was no exception. They gave her the names of the hospitals, names of local hotels, distance from the airport, everything they could think of that would possible help. When she'd typed all the information out, she tapped on the boardroom door, then slipped quietly inside to leave the note in front of Marcus. Thankfully he came out almost immediately.

'Get her for me, will you?' he said, sounding so thoroughly fed up that Toby smiled sympathetically. As he pushed through into his own office, she quickly put Wanda through to him. While he was talking she made a provisional booking for his sister on the seven o'clock flight from Heathrow, and before she had time to wonder what she should do next Dent & Co., came back with the information they'd been able to find out: the name of the hospital, and that he was in intensive care with crushed ribs and possible internal injuries. They'd also arranged for a car to be at Malta airport, and booked Wanda into a hotel. They would take care of her expenses.

'See if you can get her a flight,' Marcus rapped, coming through into her office.

'I already have. I've booked her on the 19.00 from

Terminal Two. A car will meet her the other end, and her husband's company have booked her into a hotel. He's in St George's hospital with broken ribs and possible internal injuries. Is there anything else I can do?' she asked in genuine concern, then wondered why he looked totally astonished. Did he not expect her to care? She knew she'd hardly given him a very good impression of her capabilities so far, but surely he didn't need to look dumbfounded?'

'Thank you,' he finally said, the bright blue eyes staring at her almost assessingly. Then with an impatient twitch of his expensively clad shoulders he added, 'You'd better come with me. She sounded hysterical.'

'Yes,' she murmured, lowering her lashes to hide the gleam of humour in her eyes. She couldn't quite see Marcus coping with an hysterical woman, sister or not. 'I'll lock up first.'

Nodding, he disappeared back into the board room, presumably to explain why he had to leave. By the time Toby had locked the files and her desk, alerted the chauffeur, who for once was easy to find, and collected her bag, Marcus was back.

'Does Davies know?'

'Yes. He'd downstairs with the car.'

'Right, let's go. Did Anthony's company say what had happened?' Marcus asked as they settled themselves in the back of the Daimler.

Toby was rather more conscious of the powerful thigh resting beside hers than she wanted to be, and she tried to move her legs unobtrusively away from his, which wasn't easy when he seemed to take up the whole of the back seat.

'Yes,' she murmured. 'A crane cable apparently snapped, despositing the boxes it was unloading . . .' And, not quite liking to say 'on top of Anthony', she allowed her sentence to trail off.

Murmuring something non-committal, he began tapping his fingers irritatingly on the arm-rest until Toby wanted to grab his hand and still the unconscious movements. Glancing at him from the corner of her eye, noting the frown that pulled at his dark, well-marked brows, she sighed, not sure that she wanted to be involved in his sister's drama. He'd seemed to take it rather for granted that she was able to cope, which was surprising considering he seemed to have such a low opinion of her capabilities. It was also difficult to tell if his preoccupation was with his sister's problems or at having to leave his precious board meeting. From what little she knew of him, he seemed to eat, sleep and think work at all times, and she wondered if he ever did anything for recreation, or just for the hell of it. She was inclined to strongly doubt it. That face was far too controlled. It was almost as if nature had been very meticulous in getting everything just right, with no room left for spontaneity. Impulse was most definitely not in his vocabulary, so it really must have been a mark of desperation, she thought with a little grin, that he had taken her on as his secretary.

Turning her face the other way, she stared out of her window, trying to think of what she might have left undone. Presumably Marcus would run his sister to the airport, or Davies, and that literally left her holding the baby. She hadn't even thought to ask Wanda how old it was, didn't even know what sex it was—as if that made any difference. She didn't know very much about babies.

'Do you know anything about babies?' she asked Marcus, turning back to face him.

'Babies?' he asked, sounding absolutely horrified. 'Why should I know anything about babies?'

'Well, don't you have any?'

'I sincerely hope not,' he murmured, staring at her as though she'd gone mad. 'Why did you suppose I might?'

'Well, I don't know. Most men your age are married with families. I just thought you might know something about babies.'

'Well, I don't. Neither am I married.' And the way he said it made it sound as though being married were on a par with being executed or having some infectious disease.

'Well, how old is Wanda's baby?'

'What? Oh, I see,' he said more slowly, his frown deepening. 'Oh, hell! Six months?' he asked, looking comically dismayed, before admitting, 'I don't know. Not very old, I don't think. Why? Don't you know anything about babies?'

'Not very much, no,' she said ruefully. 'I hope it's not being breast-fed, else we will be in trouble.'

'Oh, no,' he said decisively, giving her a look of horror. 'If it is, she'll have to take it with her. In fact, it might not be a bad idea for her to take it, anyway.'

'Oh, Marcus, she can't! She's worried sick about her husband. How can she cope with a baby as well? Especially if it needs regular feeds. You can't just leave babies and hope for the best, you know.'

'Well, I know that! But I can't cope with a baby! I live in a small service flat in London. I don't even have a housekeeper!'

'Well, don't you have any other family? A mother? Another sister? Sister-in-law?'

'No. Oh, hell.'

Then, as he turned toward her with a rather nasty gleam in his eyes, she held up her hands, palms toward him, and cried, 'Oh, no. Oh, no, my friend. Not me. I know absolutely nothing about babies. I barely know one end from the other.'

'Rubbish!' he said succinctly. 'All women know about babies.'

'Not this one. I don't even know anyone who's got one, let alone know how cope with it. You have to know how to change a nappy, how to bring up the wind, what strength mixture for the feed. Oh, no. I'd probably kill the poor thing off. I am not known for my domestic pursuits. I can't even cook!'

'Well, that doesn't surprise me,' he said squashingly. 'In fact, I don't know why it surprises me you don't know anything about babies. It shouldn't. I have never yet found anything you could do except drive me insane.'

Pulling a little face at him, she grinned, then turned to look out the window. 'Well, haven't you got a mother?' he asked, sounding thoroughly aggrieved.

'Yes, of course. But she lives in Edinburgh, and I hardly think she'd be delighted to have a strange baby dumped on her.' She could just imagine her mother's horrified expression if Toby arrived

with a small baby. She'd only remarried a few
months ago, and was still virtually on her
honeymoon. Apart from which, even if her mother
agreed, Toby wouldn't do that to her; her mother
needed time on her own to get to know her new
husband.

Marcus didn't speak for the rest of the journey,
just lapsed back into grumpy silence, and Toby
stared out at the passing scenery. Not that it was
particularly riveting, although Shooters Hill did
conjure up shades of Dickens from her schooldays,
and she spent contented moments picturing the old
stage-coach from a *Tale of Two Cities* struggling up
the hill in the mud. It also amused her to see that the
Anchor in Hope pub had the wrong sign outside. It
depicted a ship's anchor instead of a stage and
hitching post. It was the old stage that had anchored,
not a ship, in the hope that it didn't slip back down
the hill, which had been a great deal steeper than it
was today. Presumably it was also hoped it didn't
get attacked by highwaymen; she seemed to
remember Dick Turpin had ranged around in this
area.

As they pulled on to the motorway, Toby
speculated uselessly on where his sister might live,
and a sudden rather alarming thought occurred to
her. 'How far exactly are we going?'

'The other side of Darenth. Why?' he asked, as
though it couldn't possible matter to her one way or
the other.

'Because if it were further, Portsmouth or somewhere on the coast, there wasn't much likelihood of
my getting home tonight,' she explained patiently.

It didn't seem to occur to him that she might have a social life; just because he was married to his job didn't mean she was.

'Is it important that you do?' he asked with barely concealed indifference.

'Not especially important, no, except that I would need to let my flatmate know.'

'Oh,' he muttered grudgingly. 'Well, until I've seen Wanda and can make arrangements for the baby, I shan't know either.'

Giving a small sigh, Toby returned her attention to the scenery, barely aware that their odd relationship had changed, or that she was now calling him Marcus, as though he were a friend instead of her boss. As they turned off the motorway and drove along deserted country lanes, Toby had not the faintest idea where they were, and Marcus seemingly had no desire to enlighten her. It wasn't until they turned in between rather ornate gateposts virtually hidden by a straggly-looking hedge that he muttered, 'We're here.'

'Well, you don't need to sound as though you're going to the dentist! She is your sister,' she reproved.

'I know! But the whole thing's a damned nuisance, and quite exceptionally inconvenient.'

'Well, I'm sure Anthony didn't do it on purpose just to thwart you,' she murmured, exchanging a glance with the chauffeur, who seemed thoroughly riveted by the exchange. Glancing towards the house that suddenly came into view round the curved drive, she stared in astonishment. It looked like a damned great castle. 'Your sister lives here?' she exclaimed faintly. 'Who's she married to? The Count of Monte Cristo?'

'Don't be ridiculous!' he snapped, then climed out with marked reluctance as Davies held the door wide. Scrambling inelegantly across the seat, Toby joined Marcus on the drive, then just stood staring up at the the gargoyled portico with utter fascination.

No sooner had Davies closed the car door than the front door was flung open and a young woman who could easily have been the twin of the man beside her propelled herself down the short flight of steps and into Marcus's arms. To say that he looked startled was an understatement. Loving contact with a member of his family seemed something completely foreign to his nature, judging by his face. He also looked mortally embarrassed, or perhaps the fact that Toby and the chauffeur had witnessed the exchange had something to do with it. But, whatever the reason, he hastily urged his sister inside, leaving Toby to follow.

'I've packed,' Wanda said breathlessly, barely giving Toby a glance. 'Can we go now?'

'Not yet. The flight doesn't go until seven,' Marcus said shortly, 'Come on into the lounge,' he added, taking her elbow in what looked like a fierce grip. 'Toby, go and make some tea.'

Yes, Toby, why don't you go and make some tea? she told herself staunchly. Did you think you were here as a guest? Goodness me, no! Walking along the hall in the direction she guessed the kitchen to be, she pushed through the end door. The house might have been old, not to say ancient, but the

same could not be said for the kitchen. It looked
more like a space laboratory. Gleaming chrome and
glass everywhere that to Toby seemed totally
unsuited to the period. Filling the electric kettle at
the gleaming sink, she plugged it in before hunting
in cupboards for the teapot. There was nothing so
mundane as teabags. A silver caddy contained, if she
didn't miss her guess, Earl Grey, and the matching
sugar bowl probably contained super-refined sugar.
Feeling a bit like the upstairs maid from some Gothic
novel, she carried the naturally silver tray into the
lounge, then placed it carefully on the carved and
highly polished sideboard.

'Tea,' she announced, then spoilt it all by
grinning. As the blue eyes that were so much like her
brother's turned blankly toward her, Toby smiled
encouragingly, then relaxed slightly as she saw
comprehension slowly dawn on the drawn, white
face.

'Thank you, I . . .' Wanda began helplessly. 'I
can't seem to think straight—are you a friend of
Marcus's?'

'Not exactly,' she murmured, squashing the
temptation to look at him. Holding out her hand,
she explained, 'Toby Anderson, your brother's
secretary.'

'Temporary secretary,' Marcus corrected drily,
evincing for once a trace of humour. 'Very
temporary.' Judging by the look he was giving her,
it would be even more temporary then she
anticipated. Giving him a look of amusement, she
turned back to his sister, but before she could say
anything else a loud wail issued forth from some-

where upstairs.

'I'll see to the baby, shall I?' As Wanda just continued to stare helplessly at her, not even seeming very sure what was being said, Toby patted her shoulder comfortingly before going out. It seemed that, like that maid she had likened herself to earlier, she was neither fish nor fowl, and it was difficult to know how much or how little Marcus expected her to do. But she could hardly leave the baby to cry by itself.

Running lightly up the rather splendid staircase, she halted at the top, trying to decide which room the crying was coming from. She didn't want to go nosing around without permission, but with a small shrug, she carefully pushed open each ornately carved door on the landing until she came to the nursery. Standing in the doorway, she stared at the cot in the corner of the beautifully decorated room and a smile tugged at her mouth. The baby looked like Marcus in a temper, and could only be a boy. He had a shock of dark hair and his little face was still red from his tantrum, and screwed up into cross lines. He was about eight months old, Toby guessed, and as she entered he hauled himself up on the bars, chubby little fists clenched on the rail as he scowled at her. Then, apparently deciding she wasn't dangerous, he gave her a beaming smile that quite immediately captured Toby's tender heart.

'Hello,' she greeted softly as she walked across the tufted blue carpet, then had to hastily duck as a swinging mobile threatened to scalp her. Holding out her arms, she lifted the baby up and was surprised at how heavy he was. He was also very wet.

'Well, sunshine, I suppose I'd better change you, hadn't I? Your poor mum isn't in any fit state to be worried.' As he gurgled with laughter, she dropped a light kiss on his head, feeling, for some extra-ordinary reason, quite maternal. Seeing a pile of nappies on the white dresser that was decorated with pictures of Thumper, she walked across to collect one. She also took a pair of rubber pants from the pile alongside. Over by the window was a white bench with a sort of soft rubber cushion on it, and she laid the baby on it to remove his wet nappy, then dropped it in the white bucket beside the cot. The baby didn't seem to mind a complete stranger dealing with him, and Toby tried to remember the rather complicated fold of the other nappy as she pinned it on, then laughed as it promptly slid down when she lifted him up.

'Oh, well, perhaps the rubber pants will keep it on, mm? Tugging them on over his chubby legs, she then carried him downstairs and into the lounge. 'One changed and relatively happy baby,' she announced, pleased to see that Wanda looked a little less distressed, although the room fairly crackled with emotion. Hoping to lighten the tension, she asked with spurious gaiety, 'Have we come to any decisions regarding buster here?' She sounded like some jolly nanny, she decided in disgust, but she wasn't sure how else to deal with the situation she found herself in. It wasn't a predicament she was very used to. Seeing Wanda's faint smile, she glanced down at the large amount of nappy that was sticking out from beneath the rubbers. 'I'm not very expert,' she murmured ruefully.

'You'll soon get the hang of it,' Wanda smiled. 'I am grateful. I was in such a worry as to what to do about him, I can't tell you how much I appreciate it.'

Standing very still, Toby glanced at Marcus. He was looking at his most bland, the blue eyes totally expressionless, and she tightened her mouth fractionally, her eyes telling him exactly what she thought of his high-handedness in offering her services, especially when she'd told him quite clearly that she wouldn't do it. Opening her mouth to remonstrate with him, she closed it again. The last thing Wanda needed was a row between her brother and his secretary. 'I'll get you for this,' she whispered as she passed him to sit next to his sister, the baby on her lap. Turning to Wanda, she said, 'You'd better explain about his feeds, his routine and so on. I don't know anything about babies.'

As Wanda quickly explained, Toby was only too aware of Marcus watching her with a sardonic expression on his face which made it doubly difficult for her to take in all the instructions. 'Could you write it all down?' she asked, breaking in. 'I'm terrified I'll forget something important.'

'Yes, of course. I'll get a pen and some paper.' As she went out, Toby turned to Marcus and said softly, 'Just because I'm amiable, it doesn't mean I can be pushed around or taken for granted . . .'

'You are employed by me, in whatever capacity I choose,' he replied, equally quietly, his eyes holding hers 'Unless you wish to terminate your employment. Do you?'

'No,' she snapped shortly, feeling an uncharacteristic desire to wallop him hard, right across his smug face. She couldn't afford to terminate it.

No, I didn't think you would,' he murmured, his eyes holding the very expression she was coming to loathe. Sort of nastily amused—and he only looked away when Wanda returned. And what had he meant, anyway? He didn't know her reasons for wanting to work for him. He couldn't. Leaning back into the sofa cushions, she remained quietly pensive while Wanda wrote out the list. As the baby began investigating the buttons on the front of her dress she smiled faintly.

'There you are, I think that covers everything. I'll ring as soon as I can, and you can ask me anything you don't understand. He's very good. Well, usually,' she qualified. Then, glancing at her watch, she gave Marcus a strained smile. 'Can't we go yet?'

Nodding, he got to his feet, then looked astonished when Toby did the same. 'Are you going somewhere?' he asked pointedly.

'I don't know. Aren't I?' Toby asked lamely. 'I thought I was coming with you.'

'Well, you aren't. You're staying right here.' Turning away, he took Wanda's elbow in a firm grip. Giving his arrogant back a look of pure venom, Toby began to wonder how Sally had ever thought she had a nice nature. She didn't feel very nice. In fact she felt murderous, and if it hadn't been for the baby and Wanda's distress she would probably have said so. Sitting down again, she stared at the baby. 'Now what?' she asked him, then laughed delightedly as he blew her a raspberry. 'My sentiments exactly. Your uncle,' she told him solemnly, 'is a royal pain in the *derrière*.'

Babies, she discovered—at least, those of eight months old—did not require much looking after. She fed him, then put him back to bed where he went happily back to sleep. It was too early to ring Sally, she wouldn't be back from work yet. And how long did his lordship expect her to stay in his sister's house? It would be days at the very least, possibly a week. She would need clothes, toiletries, food. In fact, thinking about food, she realised she was starving. She hadn't had any lunch. Nor breakfast, come to that. All she'd had were a few biscuits with her morning coffee.

By the time Marcus returned at half-past eight in the evening, Toby had worked herself up into a fine told temper. She'd explored the house and part of the enormous garden, not liking to go too far from the house in case the baby woke. But from the end of the lawn she could see that not only was there a pool, but a tennis court as well. Very affluent. All right for some, she thought. When she returned to the house she explored the contents of the fridge, even the freezer. There was enough food, she supposed. In fact, to be honest, more than enough, and certainly of a quality she could never afford. Was she also supposed to do the housework? She hoped not, for it would need an army of women to keep the place clean, and domestic pursuits were not exactly what she was best known for. She'd also spent some time playing with the baby, given him his tea, inexpertly bathed him and put him back to bed.

'Where the hell have you been?' she demanded as

Marcus came through the front door, the nice nature Sally was convinced she had nowhere in evidence.

'You know where the hell I've been. Stop being so damned difficult!' he retorted, pushing past her.

'Me, difficult?' she exploded. 'I think I've been very reasonable in the circumstances!'

'You're never reasonable,' he snorted rudely, 'Is there anything to eat? I'm starving.'

'Then you should have eaten out,' she said unfeelingly. 'I've already been cast in the role of nanny; being Cook is something I don't need. Nor do I intend to start. How——'

Ruthlessly interrupting what she had been about to say, he fixed her with a cold stare, then said softly, 'You said you couldn't cook.' And when she only looked blank, he added impatiently, 'In the car, you said you couldn't cook.'

'Oh. No, I can't.'

'Domestic science is cooking, isn't it?'

Oh, knickers! She knew she shouldn't have put domestic science on that damned CV, but after stupidly telling him over the phone when she'd rung up to arrange an interview that she had eight O levels, she then couldn't think of eight and had, in desperation, come up with cooking. 'You have a good memory,' she murmured, playing for time.

'Yes, Miss Anderson, I do. Something you would do well to remember. So perhaps you would care to explain how you got an O-level in domestic science when you can't cook?' he asked silkily.

'I . . .' she began lamely, frantically trying to get her brain into overdrive, then let her breath out in relief as she heard the front door thud to.

'Saved by the bell,' he taunted, only Toby had a horrible feeling the subject wasn't by any means abandoned. As he turned away to direct Davies upstairs with his luggage, Toby surveyed his suitcase with a sour expression. About to demand what he was going to do about her own belongings, he forestalled her. As he turned back to her, no doubt reading her expression very well, judging by the nasty smile he gave, he said, 'Davies will take you to your flat so that you can collect your belongings. He will then bring you straight back here—just in case you had any idea about not doing so.'

Tempted to aim a kick at him, she went to swing past him, only to have her arm caught in a punishing grip. 'Not so fast, Miss Anderson,' he said softly.

Glaring at him, blowing irritably at an errant strand of hair that chose that particular moment to fall over her face, she waited in mutinous silence, disliking him intensely. However had she thought being grumpy was endearing? She must have been mad.

'Is the baby likely to wake up?'

'I have no idea,' she retorted sweetly, but if there was any way she could ensure just that she thought she might do so. Unfortunately, she couldn't think of anything.

'If he does, what?'

'Give him a drink?' she suggested innocently, her lovely soft mouth pursed, her eyes at their widest.

'Of?' he gritted, his jaw beginning to clench again.

'Your sister's list is in the kitchen. Why don't you read it? I had to.' She swung hastily away from him as Davies came down the stairs. She hadn't missed the bunching of his fists, and thought it might be politic to remove herself before she pushed him to the limit of his temper. But she was damned if she was going to give in meekly to his arrogance. As she reached the front door, she suddenly stopped. Swinging round again, she asked, 'Why can't I just take the baby to the flat?' It wouldn't be ideal, but it would be a great deal better than sharing this house with him.

'If you think I'm leaving my nephew with you without my supervision, you are very mistaken.'

'Why? You don't know anything about babies. You said so.'

'Neither do you,' he retorted and, turning abruptly away from her, ran lightly up the stairs.

Making an inarticulate sound of fury in the back of her throat, she stormed out to the car. Hunching crossly on the back seat, she ignored all the chauffeur's efforts to get her to talk. In the frame of mind she was in, she'd probably say something totally indiscreet. And that would only give the great Marcus du Mann something else to level at her. How on earth, she wondered, were they to co-exist in the same house without coming to blows? She'd never met anyone who so ruffled her. In fact, she hadn't even known she had a temper until she met him! Brooding about it all the way back to her flat, she finally decided that she wouldn't give him the satisfaction of letting him see how he could upset her. Even if it killed her, she vowed, she would keep calm.

CHAPTER THREE

BY THE time Toby had regaled Sally with the day's events, embroidering them slightly to make them more amusing, she'd fully recovered her sense of humour. When she'd arrived, she'd told the chauffeur to pick her up in about an hour, and that time was nearly up. She'd showered and changed into jeans and sweatshirt and she and Sally had eaten beans on toast, and by then she was feeling more her equable self. Putting her suitcase in the hall ready for collection, she gave Sally a teasing smile. 'If you read that an affluent City businessman has been foully murdered, you'll know who it is and who did it.'

'Is he affluent?' Sally asked, still amused by her friend's tales.

'I don't really know,' Toby admitted. 'I suppose so. His sister certainly is, judging by the size of the house and grounds.'

'Well, maybe you'll meet a nice wealthy farmer while you're down there, but I will miss you. You will ring me, won't you?' Let me know how you fare?'

'Sure. Hopefully Wanda's husband isn't too badly injured and she'll be back in a few days. I hope so, anyway. I don't think my nerves would stand too much of Marcus du Mann.'

'I thought you rather liked him?' Sally teased, then laughed at the disgusted face Toby pulled.

'So did I. How on earth are we going to manage not to kill each other? It was bad enough in the office, but seeing him virtually twenty-four hours a day . . .' Shaking her head ruefully, she gave Sally a quick hug as the doorbell rang. 'That will be Davies. Take care.'

'You're the one who needs to take care, not me.' Then, seeing the guitar propped against Toby's suitcase, she exclaimed, 'You're not taking that thing, are you?'

'Yes, of course. It will be a good chance to do some practice. I expect, *hope,* that the baby will sleep quite a lot, so it will be a good opportunity to master it.' She was quite unoffended when Sally burst out laughing.

'Master it? Is that what you call that awful noise that sounds as though you're strangling a cat?'

'Ah, but by the time I come back, I shall sound like Segovia, you'll see.'

Allowing Davies to take the suitcase, and carrying the guitar herself, she accompanied him down to the car. When they arrived back at the house, it was to find Marcus ensconced in the little front room that was obviously used as a study. He didn't bother to come out and greet her, so it was left to Toby to seek him out.

'Which room am I to use?' she asked bluntly, surveying the broad shirt-clad shoulders for a moment. It was the first time she'd seen him without his jacket—not that it made him look less formal; it didn't.

'Wanda said to use the one next to the nursery. It has a connecting door. I'll naturally use the master bedroom,' he said flatly without lifting his head.

'Naturally,' she murmured mildly as she closed the

door. Directing Davies up the stairs with her suitcase, she wondered with a spurt of amusement whether she was to stay in her room. Unpacking her belongings, she then put them away in the lavender-scented wardrobe. It was a pleasant room, overlooking the grounds at the rear. Decorated in muted shades of blue, similar to the nursery, it was ideal for a nanny. Suddenly she wondered why, with their obvious affluence, they didn't have one. Or maybe that was presumptuous of her, maybe Wanda preferred to take care of the baby herself, which was perhaps why the bed had already been made up. With her husband away, perhaps she'd been sleeping in this room; she didn't for one moment imagine that Marcus had done it.

Placing the *Guitar for Beginners* book on the bedside-table and propping the instrument in the corner, she went downstairs into the lounge. Turning on the television, she curled up on the sofa, debating whether to make a cup of coffee and go to bed. It was half-past eleven, so she supposed she might as well. Not knowing what time the baby might wake up, she thought it might be wise to get all the sleep she could. Turning off the television, she went into the kitchen and her lips tightened at the sight of the dirty plate and cup on the draining-board. Marcus had obviously fed himself. Well, if he thought she was going to wash up for him, he was mistaken. Putting the kettle on and getting out a cup and saucer, she suddenly remembered the tea she had made earlier and that no one had drunk. The thought of what cold tea would do to fine silver had her hastening back to the lounge. The tray was still on the sideboard where she had left it. Carrying it back to the kitchen, she emptied the teapot, then, running hot water into the sink and squirting in plenty of washing-up liquid, she carefully washed it. It seemed petty not to wash his things while she was washing up anyway, so she did those as well. Not that that meant she would do so in future, she promised herself.

Deciding it was probably also petty not to ask him if he wanted a drink, she poked her head inside. 'Do you want some coffee? I'm just making some.'

Throwing down his pen, he leaned back in the brown leather swivel chair, and Toby noticed that his face was etched in lines of strain. He looked tired, too, and she felt a swift stab of compunction for her earlier behaviour. No doubt he was worried about his brother-in-law. Going further into the room, she asked kindly, 'Is there anything I can do?' then wished she had kept quiet as his eyes widened in astonishment.

'Such as?'

Placing her hands on her hips, she surveyed him silently for a moment. Observing the tousled hair that was usually so ruthlessly suppressed, the loosened tie, the top button of his shirt undone, she said quietly, 'You really are a bastard, aren't you? I was trying to be helpful.'

'Why?' he asked bluntly.

'Why?' she asked, astonished, her unusual amber eyes at their widest. Then, with a small smile tugging at her mouth, she offered, 'Because I have a nice nature?'

He held her gaze for such a long time that she thought he wasn't going to answer. Finally, he picked up his pen and said flatly, 'Go to bed, Miss Anderson.

I'm not in the mood for your games.'

'I wasn't aware I was playing any,' she returned mildly, her eyes puzzled. 'I merely asked if you wanted some coffee. However, please yourself.' She shrugged. As she turned away to the door, she suddenly remembered something she wanted to ask him. 'By the way, am I still getting paid the same?'

'Go to bed, Miss Anderson,' he repeated wearily without looking up. 'We'll discuss it in the morning.'

Staring at his downbent head for a moment, at the dark, silky hair that shone with health despite its ruffled state, she hovered in the doorway, trying to work out what it was about him that made him so attractive to her. Normally someone who had such a lousy personality would have put her off at the first meeting. Yet it hadn't, and she had the sudden fanciful wish that he would smile. Really smile. It would make an awful lot of difference, she thought.

It wasn't a face that was classically handsome, more sort of carved, as though nature had been very careful not to put anything out of symmetry. A still face, without expression—and yet it had exceptional beauty. There were no laughter lines at the eyes, only carved grooves from nose to the corner of his mouth and a deep groove where he persisted in frowning, and Toby had the irrational desire to smooth it away. As he looked up, piercing her with those bright eyes, she hastily backed out. Heavens, for a moment there she had actually softened towards him. Definitely cracking up, Toby, she muttered to herself as she walked thoughtfully along to the kitchen. Making her coffee she then took it upstairs with her.

When she had undressed, washed and climbed into

bed and had her coffee cradled in her hands, she made
a consciouis effort to relax, unwind after the
extraordinary events of the day. Other people seemed
to manage their lives so much better than she did.
Hers seemed to muddle along, sending her in
directions she didn't particularly want to go. Look at
her behaviour today. She had quite categorically stated
in the car that she would not look after Wanda's baby,
and what was she doing? Looking after the baby. She
recalled, too, Marcus's odd words about her leaving.
What was it that he thought he knew about her?
Shaking her head in confusion, she turned out the
lamp and snuggled down under the covers. An owl
was hooting mournfully somewhere, and she shivered,
picturing the poor prey he was hunting.

Here there were no night noise likes in Blackheath,
no late-night revellers, no traffic, just the owl. And
Marcus downstairs, working in the study. Because of
her inefficiency? she wondered guiltily. Giving a long
sigh, she closed her eyes.

The sound of the baby chortling and banging his cot
against the wall woke her next morning, and Toby lay
for a few minutes orientating herself. Yawning widely,
she climbed reluctantly out of the warm bed. Not
bothering to put a robe over her white lawn nightdress
that left very little of her shape to the imagination, she
stumbled sleepily into the nursery just as Marcus
walked in from the landing. Their eyes met, tangled,
held—and something happened. Toby wasn't exactly
sure what. A spark, a knowledge, something, and for
an infinitesimal moment his eyes held surprise. They
both turned away at the same moment, Toby to pick

up the baby, Marcus to idly finger the pile of nappies on the dresser. With her hair curling riotously round her gamine face, she stared blankly at the baby. If anyone had wanted to test her, she could have told them exactly, down to the tiniest detail, how Marcus looked. What he wore, the amount of stubble on his chin. The short navy towelling robe barely covered his strong thighs, and she felt a very peculiar dip in her stomach as she realised he was probably naked beneath it.

'Good morning,' she mumbled huskily, amazed to find that she was actually embarrassed.

'Don't you have a robe?' he demanded.

'What?' she mumbled, reluctantly turning her head to stare at him. As his words registered she looked down at herself, then hastily held the baby in front of her in a belated effort to cover up the parts she was exposing. 'I'm not at my best at this ungodly hour,' she explained lamely—then, as the baby grabbed a handful of hair and laughed delightedly, she thankfully returned her attention to him. 'And what do you find so funny? It's early,' she told him with mock severity.

'Oh, for God's sake!' Marcus snapped as he stormed out, slamming the door behind him.

Letting her breath out in a whoosh, Toby relaxed the muscles she hadn't been aware she'd been holding rigid. Well, that *would* be clever, Toby. Fancy him, why don't you? 'Nonsense,' she said out loud. Hastily banishing his image from her mind, she turned her attention to the baby. 'Come on, then, let's get you changed.'

When she'd washed and changed him in the little en suite bathroom, she dressed him in a blue romper-suit that she found in one of the drawers. Carrying him back to her bedroom, she put him in the middle of the bed while she unearthed her robe from the wardrobe.

Marcus was sitting at the kitchen table when she went down, a cup nursed between his large palms. He was still wearing the navy towelling robe he'd had on earlier, yet even being unshaven and half naked didn't make him seem any more approachable. Sexy, she decided, but definitely unapproachable. But at least her stupid awareness of him had gone, she thought thankfully, and she was able to ignore that bright glance that travelled insultingly from the top of her head to her feet. Well, almost ignore, she qualified. A little frivolity in his nature wouldn't come amiss, and she wondered with a little spurt of amusement if he even made love by numbers, then hastily banished the thought. Images of Marcus making love in any way at all were definitely not to be dwelt on. 'Any tea in the pot?' she managed to ask more or less evenly.

As he pushed the teapot across, he continued to stare at her, an expression of distaste marring the well-shaped mouth, and Toby turned quickly away to collect a cup for herself and fill the baby's feeder-cup with milk. Putting the kettle on, she got out the box of Farex, then tipped a liberal amount into a bowl. As she poured the boiling water on to it, she grimaced. It had the colour and consistency of porridge, and, if there was one thing that made her feel positively ill, it was porridge. Returning to the table, she sat next to the high chair, then proceeded to blow on each spoonful before giving it to the baby.

'Not very hygienic,' he commented disagreeably.

Giving a little snort of exasperation, she pushed

the bowl toward him, bringing forth an impatient howl from the baby. 'You want to do it?' she asked.

'No.'

'Then keep your opinions to yourself.' Scraping up the last of the cereal, she laughed delightedly as the baby blew a raspberry at Marcus, spraying minute portions of his breakfast to sprinkle the dark hair. Hastily she straightened her face when he glared at her.

'Does he have to do that?' he snapped, pushing his hand across his hair to wipe off the mess.

'Of course he does. Babies like blowing raspberries,' she explained sweetly. Then, tipping her head on one side, she asked, 'What's his name?' I can't keep calling him "baby".'

'Peter,' he said shortly.

'Well, Peter,' she murmured, getting up again, quite oblivious to the fact that her robe gaped open at the front, giving Marcus a fine view of softly rounded breasts, 'pram time. Keep an eye on him, will you, while I get the pram out?' And without waiting for an answer she walked out into the conservatory where Wanda kept the pram. Pushing it out into the garden, she then went back for the baby. Wiping his hands and face, she then carrried him outside for his sleep, making sure his harness was securely fastened before going back inside. Sitting back at the table, she poured herself a cup of tea, then, holding it in front of her, surveyed Marcus over the rim.

'I do wish you wouldn't look so bad-tempered,' she said mildly. 'It's very off-putting.'

'Tough,' he said unfeelingly. 'Although I strongly doubt that anything, short of being rendered unconscious, would put you off—and I gather that all this has some point?'

'Yes. I wanted to ask you if I'm to get the same money for looking after the house and ba . . .' She jumped in alarm as Marcus slammed his cup down, his blue eyes positively blazing with temper.

'You have a preoccupation with money that borders on the unhealthy!' he snapped scathingly.

Giving him a look of astonishment, she began lamely, 'I only meant . . .'

'I know what you only meant!'

She didn't think he did, but now didn't seem the time to point it out, so she said instead, 'Only the wealthy can afford to make such statements with equanimity. When you're poor, money matters. We don't all have a healthy bank balance, you know.' And hers seemed perpetually less healthy than most. She'd only wanted to know if she was to be paid less.

Ignoring her taunts, he said flatly, 'A Mrs Henson comes in each day to clean. No doubt, for a little extra,' he added nastily, a sneer pulling at his mouth, which only went to prove that he had misunderstood her, 'she would be willing to prepare the meals and give you a hand with the baby.'

'Leave me free to do what?' she asked softly, her eyes gleaming with laughter.

'What I pay you for, Miss Anderson. Typing my reports. I've asked Davies to bring the typewriter down here.'

'Ah.' After taking a few sips of her tea, her eyes still holding his, she murmured, 'Perhaps she would also be willing to look after Peter all the time, then you wouldn't have to have my tiresome presence in the house.'

'She won't. I already asked her.' Giving her a look that she could only call impudent, he got to his feet, adding, 'I'm going to shower and dress. I suggest you do the same. Or did you intend to float around like that all day?'

Tempted to give him a sarcastic rejoinder, she changed her mind, and just stared at him, her eyes widened innocently, which thoroughly infuriated him. As he stormed out, she gave a little *moue* of disgust at his retreating back. Well, whatever else their sojourn under the same roof would be, it wouldn't be boring. Fraught maybe, but not boring.

Davies arrived an hour later with her typewriter, followed soon after by Mrs Henson, who turned out to be as thin as a stick, with grey hair scragged back unflatteringly into a tight bun. She looked formidable, and well able to cope with Marcus at his worst, she guessed. Giving her a warm smile that was reciprocated with a look of suspicion, Toby checked on the baby before presenting herself in the study. Marcus was now very firmly encased in his City armour. A navy suit this time, which again fitted him to perfection and made his eyes seem bluer, brighter. He was rifling impatiently through his briefcase, his movements less than controlled. Did everything drive him into fury? Or was it only herself? Only herself, she decided as he gave her a look of utter despondency.

'I suppose it's no good asking you what happened to the reports you typed on Monday?' he asked with the obvious expectation of her denial.

'I attached them to the accounts, as you requested,'

she murmured with a little twinkle of amusement. 'They're in the brown folder in the cupboard in my office. On top—truly,' she added when he only continued to stare at her in disbelief, then gave a gurgle of laughter as he grimaced. He actually looked quite human for a change, and she smiled warmly at him. 'Not totally useless, you see.'

'Really?' he asked drily. 'You mean there might actually be hope that one day you'll be able to anticipate my needs? Remember where you put things?'

'There is absolutely no need to be sarcastic, Marcus,' she said, laughing. 'I'm improving by the minute.'

Giving her a glance of pure disbelief, he shook his head, then, obviously remembering his need for haste, quickly checked his watch. 'I have to go up to Leeds. Davies is running me to the airport to catch the ten-thirty, but if all goes well with the meeting, I should be back about five-thirty. I've left a list of things to be done on my desk. If you have problems ring Frank Dawson. And I mean that, Toby. Don't go making decisions off your own bat!'

'I won't,' she murmured meekly. 'Have a nice day.' For some reason the last comment actually made him laugh. Grudging, but definitely a laugh of sorts.

Smiling softly to herself, she turned to pick up the list, and then gave a little grunt of laughter. It was very comprehensive. A report to be retyped, telephone calls to be made altering his schedule to fit in with his self-imposed need to be at home each evening. He obviously thought she was likely to do irreparable damage to his nephew if either Mrs Henson or himself were not around to prevent it. He also wanted a report drafted out from the list of salient points jotted on the pad in his bold, slashing writing.

Unlike the office, where there were other people to answer the phone, which seemed to ring incessantly, here there was only herself. Mrs H had taken herself off to the shops and Toby was left to cope with the oil delivery, the vicar, who had only just heard of Anthony's accident, and the local man who supplemented his income by doing people's gardens and who seemed to find it necessary to regale Toby with tales of his adventures. Then, to cap it all, a woman from the Women's Institute called collecting jumble. Marcus was never going to believe that her day had been so full that she'd barely had time to type his reports, she thought wryly. Then, just as she'd settled down after a sketchy lunch, having put the baby back down for a nap, the window cleaner arrived, which left her in the embarrassing position of not being able to pay him. She had precisely sixty-seven pence in her purse. Explaining the problem, she asked if he could possibly call back later.

When Marcus returned at just gone five, Toby was at crawling round the living-room floor with Peter. As she heard the door open, she turned a laughing face toward him, exclaiming, 'Hello! You're nice and early.' And she thought, just for a moment, that he was going to smile, but then he obviously changed his mind, which was a pity, she thought. She'd like him to smile. Looking tousled and very young, she sat back on her heels. 'Bad day?' she asked gently.

Staring at her, his eyes taking in the tight jeans, the shirt half in and half out of the waistband, he murmured wryly, 'Since the very first morning that you walked into my life, my days have got progressively worse. Why should this one be any different?' Then, giving a long sigh, he added, 'When you've finished whatever it is you're doing, perhaps you'd come into the study.'

Tempted to emulate Peter and blow him a raspberry, a fact he was very well aware of, judging by his expression, she grinned disarmingly. 'We were playing tigers,' she explained solemnly. 'Nothing which can't be postponed.' She gave a little chuckle as he turned and walked out. Getting to her feet and lifting Peter into her arms, she walked to the study, the baby balanced on one hip. Marcus was reading the report she'd typed, his mouth tight, no trace at all of the almost wry humour he had evinced earlier. As he finished, he looked up, and it would hardly have taken a genius to know what he thought of her efforts.

'I find it very hard to comprehend,' he began slowly, tossing the pages back toward her, 'how on earth you ever managed to pass your O levels, never mind the As. I wanted, needed an edited report in a comprehensive form that is both pertinent and short. What I did not need was a damned novel!'

Opening her mouth, not quite sure if she was going to remonstrate or apologise, she closed it again as someone tapped impatiently on the window. 'The window cleaner,' she explained on recognising the man.

'Well, tell him to come back later,' he said impatiently, glaring at her.

'It is later,' she explained softly. 'And I need eight pounds and fifty pence. I didn't have enough money to pay him earlier.'

'Miss Anderson,' he gritted as she walked across to open the window, 'I have far more important things to think of at the moment than the payment of the window cleaner. Tell him to come back on Saturday.'

'No,' Toby said mildly, miming to the window cleaner to hang on a minute. Turning back to Marcus, she explained kindly. 'He might need the oney today . . .'

'It's only eight pounds fifty, for God's sake!' he exploded.

'. . . and if everyone deferred payment,' she continued, ignoring his violent interuption, 'he might not be able to last until Saturday. He might need petrol, food for his family. It might be only eight pounds fifty to you, but to him it might be the difference between eating tonight or starving.' As she knew only too well from when people hadn't paid her father on time.

'All right, all right,' he said, holding his hands up in defeat. Delving into his inside pocket, he produced his wallet, from which he extracted a ten-pound note.

'Thank you,' she murmured, taking it from him and walking across to hand it to the cleaner. When she returned, she solemnly handed over his change.

'May we now get on?'

'Yes, of course, but will it take very long? Only I have to bath buster here and put him to bed.'

'Can't Mrs Henson do it?'

'No. She's cooking dinner—she's a bit fierce, isn't she?' she added, shifting the baby into a more comfortable postion. 'I'd be almost too . . .'

'Miss Anderson!' he yelled, and, when she lapsed

into startled silence, continued through his teeth, 'I do not want, neither do I need, a dissertation on the character of Mrs Henson! What I want, *need*, is a secretary who at least tries to give the impression of alert interest.'

'Well, I was only saying . . .'

'I know what you were only saying,' he muttered grimly, then transferred his attention to the baby, who was happily undoing the buttons on the front of her shirt. Letting his breath out in exasperation, he said, 'Go and bath the baby. We'll work after dinner.'

'All right,' she agreed. 'And I am sorry about the report. I really was trying.' Disentangling Peter's chubby fingers from her buttons, she sighed and moved to the door, then came to a halt. 'Would you like to bath him?' She gave a little grimace as he buried his face in his hands. 'You might enjoy it,' she encouraged. 'It would relax you. You work too hard, you know.'

'Well, one of us needs to! Oh, just go and bath him,' he added wearily.

Walking thoughtfully upstairs and into the nursery bathrooom, she perched on the edge of the bath while she ran the water. 'Oh, Peter, what is poor old Toby to do?' Smiling ruefully, she dropped a kiss on the downy hair. 'Get a bit of a shock if you answered me, wouldn't I?' As soon as the water was ready, she undressed him and, kneeling, held him safely in the water. She liked bath time, she could behave as childishly as she pleased with no one to look askance at her silly behaviour. Water splashing and duck throwing was tremendous fun. Laughing delightedly as Peter threw the wet sponge at her with great accuracy for an eight-month-old baby, she suddenly became aware of being watched. Slowly turning her head, she grinned lamely at Marcus, who was leaning in the doorway. He looked almost wistful, she thought in surprise. A look that was gone as quickly as it had materialised.

'Change your mind?' she asked softly.

'No.' Yet his voice was slightly husky, and he had to clear his throat before continuing. 'No,' he said again more strongly. 'I came to ask if you'd made that appointment with Recvens.'

'Reevens? Oh, yes. Seven-thirty at the Savoy on Thursday. I left a note on your desk. He asked if you wanted to go on to Annabel's afterwards. Would you let him know in the morning?'

Nodding, he smiled faintly as Peter brought both chubby hands down flat on the water, soaking Toby further. 'You look as though you need a wet-suit for that operation.' Then, giving her an odd look, he turned and went out.

The man was becoming more and more of an enigma, mused Tony. Did he long to marry and have a family? she wondered. Certainly his look seemed to suggest something along those lines. Realising how cool the water was getting, she lifted Peter out and wrapped him in a fluffy towel. As soon as she laid him down, he was asleep. Smiling down at the innocent face, she then went to wash and change for dinner.

Replacing the jeans and shirt with a soft pink cotton dress, she put on the minimum of making-up before going back down. She poked her head into the kitchen to see if Mrs H needed any help, and on receiving her denial she wandered into the lounge. Switching on the television to catch the end of the news, she plumped down on to the sofa. Only, instead of taking in the images on the screen, her mind was filled with thoughts of Marcus. It seemed as if he was afraid to relax, let himself go, and she wondered why. Perhaps he was afraid she'd become too familiar. Take advantage. Or was there something in his background that had made him wary of relationships? It surely wasn't only herself, although she knew she infuriated him; but at work he never let his guard drop like the other directors. Even Sir David, who presumably had far more reason to keep himself distant—a man of his wealth and position would be bound to attract hangers on—yet he wasn't. He was friendly and seemed interested in other people. So what had made Marcus so afraid to reveal himself? Even with his sister he'd been stiff, unnatural, afraid almost to use the word love. Or had nothing made him like it? Was it just his natural behaviour? Even as a child? Withdrawn, wary? It wasn't anything as simple as shyness, because he certainly wasn't that. He was arrogant, insulting, intolerant, and yet once or twice today he'd been quite friendly. It was almost as if he was putting on an act, afraid to let her see him for what he was.

'Dinner,' Mrs Henson announced from the doorway.

'Mm? Oh, OK, thanks, Mrs H,' Toby said easily, getting to her feet. And there was another one with the barriers very firmly up, she thought ruefully. Was she afraid Toby would transgress on her preserves? Ask awkward questions? Perhaps she thought Toby would be the catalyst. Smiling to herself, she went into the dining-room. Taking the place Mrs Henson indicated, she smiled as Marcus came in, determined to be friendly. A determination that became more and more strained. After his almost human behaviour, he had now retreated behind that cold mask he had worn in the office, and it was becoming something of a challenge to her to make him smile properly at least once before she left.

'Have you heard from Wanda?' she asked, shaking her napkin out and laying it neatly on her lap.

'No,' he said bluntly.

'Oh, well, perhaps she'll ring tonight.'

'Perhaps.'

'The baby's very good,' she prattled on in an effort to make him relax. 'He went straight off to sleep.' When Marcus didn't answer, she described her day in minute detail, which took them through the soup and main course, elaborating and exaggerating to make the incidents more amusing. At least *she* found them amusing, so too did Mrs Henson, judging by the twitch of her lips that she didn't have time to disguise when Toby glanced at her. Transferring her gaze to Marcus, she peeped at him from beneath her lashes. It was like trying to make a dent in rock. You could chip away, bit by bit, but only find more rock underneath. Although perhaps he just found her light-hearted chatter infuriating; maybe he wanted, needed someone who could intelligently discuss his day. Which she couldn't, or not in any great detail; she hadn't been with the firm long enough to know all the ins and outs of his business. It wasn't that she was stupid, but she didn't really know enough of what he did to make a useful contribution.

Lapsing into silence, she ate her lemon meringue,

her thoughts turning inward. She must remember to ring Sally in the morning, and she still hadn't resolved the problem of what she was to be paid. Perhaps she could ask Marcus again after dinner; she really did need to know so that she could budget accordingly. Barely noticing that her dish was removed or that coffee had been placed before her, she continued to gaze blankly ahead of her, totally unware that Marcus was speaking until his shout made her jump.

'You are totally infuriating, do you know that?' he asked angrily, getting to his feet and throwing his napkin down in disgust. 'Would it be too much to ask that you at least look as though you're paying attention when I'm talking to you, instead of gazing blankly past me with your eyes glazed?'

Blinking up at him in astonishment, her eyes holding an expression of bewildered innocence, she apologised softly. 'I'm sorry. I didn't mean to be rude. What did you say?'

His face hard, he stared at her and he looked as though he was contemplating many and varied ways of murdering her. Bending forward, his hands flat on the table, he bit out. 'You are driving me insane! Do you know that? A few more days of your company and I will be certifiable!' Snapping upright, he walked out, slamming the door behind him.

'Well,' she murmured lamely, letting her breath out in a whoosh. Staring rather blankly at the closed door that still seemed to be quivering from his rough treatment, Toby considered his words, really considered them. Turned them over and over in her head. She wasn't used to being disliked, and it hurt, she found. Yet wasn't his outburst in some ways justified? She had been treating the whole thing, not as a joke exactly, but certainly lightly. When she'd embarked on this masquerade, she hadn't for one moment considered the matter from his point of view. Hadn't really given a moment's thought to what it would do to his day if he had a useless secretary. She'd accepted thing as they'd come, coped as best she could, answered phone calls without fully understanding how delicate were the negotiations for the current takeover they were contemplating. In fact, Toby, you have been incredibly selfish, she told herself.

Was it any wonder he got in a temper with her? Was it any wonder he looked tired? As he'd said, he needed someone to take some of the load off his shoulders, and all she had considered was that she needed to pay the rent and to hell with everyone else. Exchanging a glance with Mrs Henson, her face mirroring her guilt, Toby finished her coffee before walking through to the lounge. After wandering aimlessly back and forth for a few minutes, barely taking in the exquisite ornaments and pictures that decorated the red room as she had dubbed it because of the red velvet hangings with their gold tassels, she finally walked out and across to the study. Tapping perfunctorily on the door, she poked her head inside.

Marcus was standing at the window, his back to the room, and he didn't even bother to turn at her entrance.

'I am sorry, Marcus,' she said quietly. 'I truly don't mean to infuriate you. I will try harder, I promise.' When he didn't answer, only continued his contemplation of the garden, which with dusk falling had taken on a lavender hue, Toby walked further into the room. Standing by the desk, she played idly with the ornate pen set that sat proudly on the tooled leather top. The golden eagle that made up the desk-lamp seemed to glare balefully at her and she pulled a little face at it. 'Do you want me to re-do the report?' she asked, turning to look at him. His hands were clasped behind that ramrod-straight back, his head erect, giving an added appearance of arrogance, and Toby began to feel a bit like a naughty pupil confronted by the head. Only she had to admit, he was more than justified in being angry with her. In fact, thinking about it further, in the circumstances, he'd been tolerant.

'No,' he said abruptly, then gave a long sigh as he slowly turned to face her. With the dim light behind him, leaving his face in shadow, it was hard for Toby to read his expression; only the bright blue eyes seemed to have life. 'You seem to be getting on with Peter all right,' he observed moodily, then continued to just stare at her, as though not quite sure what to do with her. Or about her, she guessed.

'Oh, yes. He's adorable. He looks a bit like you, don't you think?' she asked in an effort to lighten the rather heavy atmosphere.

'Does he?'

'Yes.'

'Especially when he scowls?' Marcus murmured, totally astonishing Toby with the sudden quirk of humour. That was twice in one day. Leaning back against the windowsill, he folded his arms across his chest. 'Perhaps you ought to redirect your energies into becoming a nanny,' he observed wryly. 'You seem more suited to it than being a secretary.'

'Not doing too well, am I?' she asked ruefully.

'No, Miss Anderson, not very well at all. Although I don't suppose it's entirely your fault.'

Widening her eyes in surprise that he should at least partially assume responsibility, she murmured magnanimously, 'Well, you have had a lot on your mind, and I expect it's six of one and half a dozen of the other.' Then she stared at him in further astonishment as he gave a snort of laughter.

'That wasn't quite what I meant,' he said drily.

'Oh,' Toby said lamely, her brow furrowing as she tried to work out what he had meant. 'Because I'm not very clever, do you mean?'

'No. I doubt there's very much wrong with your brain, just that you don't utilise it. You don't look ahead, do you? It's all *now* with you. Speculation and assumption instead of rationlisation and forward planning.'

'Now you sound like a pompous professor,' she muttered, yet had to admit that he was right. He'd summed her up very well. That was quite exactly what she did. 'You'd get on well with my mother,' she murmured with a wry little grimace. ' "Look before you leap, Toby." '

' . . . otherwise one of these days you'll get yourself into real trouble?' he finished for her, one eyebrow lifting, and as she gave a little nod he levered himself away from the window. Coming to stand before her, he looked own into her rueful face. 'Do you by any chance play backgammon?' he asked unexpectedly.

CHAPTER FOUR

'BACKGAMMON?' queried Toby faintly. Searching his face, she tried to decide if he had an ulterior motive for asking the question but, as usual, found she couldn't read his face at all. 'Not as well as you, I expect,' she admitted cautiously, 'but yes, I can play.'

'Then shall we try to find some common ground on which to operate? We seem to be stuck with each other, for the next few days at least, a situation no more appealing to you than myself, I imagine.'

Wrinkling her nose at him, she gave a gurgle of laughter before remonstrating, 'You didn't need to add the rider. That was just plain nasty.' And, giving him a teasing look that made his eyes narrow, she preceded him from the study. She felt almost light-hearted now that they were no longer at odds with each other, yet in her usual fashion didn't bother to probe the reason. It was sufficient for the moment that he was no longer angry.

As he set up the leather case on the coffee-table, Toby elected to sit on the floor, her favourite position. Removing her shoes, she curled her legs under her and, her gamine face filled with its customary enthusiasm, she picked up the leather shaker.

Marcus did beat her, but only just, which seemed to surprise him because he stared at her long and thoughtfully for a few moments, as though only just

74

seeing her as a person. 'Not as stupid as you make out, are you?' he asked softly. 'Want to make it more interesting?'

'How interesting?' Toby queried with a grin, not sure whether to feel insulted or flattered by his observation. It might also be as well to get the ground rules sorted out because, despite his opinion, she wasn't that impulsive and, after all, she didn't know him very well, yet the way he had asked it started a curl of excitement in the pit of her stomach and she was quite unable to stop the blush that stained her cheeks.

'Penny a point?'

'How many points either wins by? Or the number of points the winner gets?'

'Wins by. After the window cleaner incidents, I gather your finances are rather shaky.'

'But I intend to win,' Toby exclaimed with a grin. Then, remembering his undoubted skill, she added, 'But just in case I don't, by the number of points difference.'

'Wise girl. Red or white?'

'Red, please.'

'Figures,' he murmured, slanting her a wry look.

He did beat her, but again only by a small margin. They played another two games but, when Toby gave an enormous yawn that she was unable to stifle, he murmured, 'Bed. You can get your revenge another night.' As he got up to put the board away, Toby stared across at him. With his jacket removed and his tie loosened, he looked more approachable, unlike the day before in his study. His hair, too, was rather attractively tousled and, as he turned, as though aware of being watched, Toby blushed again. As a gleam of amusement appeared in his eyes, Toby gave a little grimace before getting agilely to her feet.

'Little, aren't you?' he observed, coming to stand in front of her.

'I haven't got my shoes on,' she said foolishly. 'And you are very tall.' He was also looking at her very oddly, and Toby was rather too aware of the appearance she must present. Her hair had once again escaped it confinement, she could feel several strands tickling her neck and cheek, and she resisted the desire to put her hands up and tidy it. It also seemed rather important to know what he was thinking. Raising her eyebrows in query, she grinned when he shook his head.

'Why is it, Miss Anderson, that every time I look at you, I get this rather ominous feeling of doom?'

'Doom?' she gurgled. 'Oh, surely not?' Then, deciding it might be wise to leave while they were still on amicable terms, she smiled again before bending to pick up her shoes. Calling goodnight, she went up to her room, her mind filled with this rather nice Marcus. Throwing her shoes on the floor, she went to gaze out of the window. He'd been really nice, and Toby made herself a mental promise that she really would try extra hard not to infuriate him. She would master the type-writer, and even, she decided, buy herself a shorthand book. Smiling to herself, knowing that her resolutions would in all probability fall far short of his expectations, she got ready for bed. He *had* been nice, though.

Marcus had already left when she went down with

Peter the next morning and, as he hadn't left her very much to do, she offered to walk, to the village to get any shopping Mrs H might need. She was wearing jeans and a T-shirt and thonged sandals, and the mile walk to the village took her far longer than she expected. People kept stopping her to admire the baby or enquire about Wanda's husband and, without being rude, Toby had no option but to answer them. In truth, she didn't really mind; being gregarious, she was rather enjoying this change in her routine, and wasn't in the least offended by questions put about herself. She thought she might quite like to live in the country. Everyone was really friendly. It was as she walked back that she overheard two elderly women gossiping, and the snatches of conversation so riveted her that she very naughtily slowed her pace to listen.

'Lydia's back, I see.'

'Aye. That'll set the cat among the pigeons.'

'Wonder if he knows?' And it was said so archly that Toby became thoroughly intrigued. It was almost as if they were discussing some forthcoming entertainment. Who was Lydia? The tall, elegant blonde, who had been in the post office? She'd looked as though she might be a Lydia—arrogant and disdainful. Yet what on earth had she done to make both women speculate so gleefully? As they passed out of earshot, Toby wondered how she could find out. It was no good asking Mrs Henson, or at least not outright.

Walking thoughtfully back to the house, she left the pram parked in the garden, and went into the kitchen. Leaning casually against the table, her lovely eyes at their most most innocent, she repeated the conversation that she had overheard almost verbatim

'Lydia's back, I see.'

'So I hear, so I hear,' Mrs H sniffed, her hand not slacking their pace as she peeled potatoes.

'Does he know?' she murmured innocently, having absolutely no idea who 'he' was. God, she was getting positively Machiavellian!

'Don't know. Wouldn't say if he did, would he?'

'Probably not,' Toby grinned, beginning to enjoy herself hugely. 'Still, it'll set the cat among the pigeons, won't it?'

'Aye.' Mrs H sighed. 'But I'll not be the one to tell him, and if you've any sense, you won't, either.'

'Oh, I don't know. Shouldn't he be warned, don't you think?' A statement which so astonished Mrs H that she actually stopped peeling.

'You'd tell him?' she exclaimed. 'Well, you've more courage than I have. Especially as you're perpetually in his bad books as it it.'

Marcus? She thought, turning her face away so that the housekeeper wouldn't see her frown. Was that who they were talking about? It certainly seemed so. So who was Lydia? A past love? But if she was, why would they say she was back? Being back pre-supposed that she had gone away, and if she'd lived here before, how had Marcus met her? Through his sister? Maybe that accounted for his odd reluctance when he'd met Wanda. That was the trouble with being devious, she decided, she couldn't now ask for an explanation, because Mrs H thought she knew and would be furious if she thought she'd been indiscreet.

'Maybe you're right,' she murmured, walking out to the garden to bring the baby in. 'It would probably end up my fault.'

'Probably,' Mrs H chuckled. 'You do seem to have the unhappy knack of rubbing him up the wrong way. Although it's not altogether your fault; it's partly the house. He always hated it. Swore he'd never come back here. But there you are, fate sometimes take a malicious delight in thwarting plans.'

Well, there was food for thought, Toby mused, her vivid imagination working overtime. That had to be the longest speech Mrs H had ever uttered. Absently fitting the baby into his high chair, Toby then went to mix his lunch, her mind busily trying to come up with ideas as to why Marcus hated the house. 'Wanda doesn't seem to mind it, though,' she murmured, almost to herself.

'Well, she wouldn't, would she? She was the old man's darling. His little angel.'

'And Marcus the devil?' Toby speculated, her voice soft and rather sad as she pictured a diminutive replica of Marcus being hounded by an evil father. Or maybe even stepfather.

'Aye, poor lad. He had the temper on him, though, just like his Dad.'

Spooning food into Peter's mouth without any real conscious thought of what she was doing, Toby only came out of her reverie when Peter spat out the last mouthful. 'Don't do that,' she scolded, then laughed as the baby beamed unrepentantly at her. 'Come on, one more, then you can have your pudding.' So, how did she now find out the rest? Toby wondered. Ask Marcus? That didn't seem a very wise move in the circumstances. Only, she really would like to know. Not from any reasons of just idle curiosity, she told herself firmly, but if she had misjudged him that was a reason to find out, wasn't it? And was that why his temper seemed to smoulder and never erupt? Because he'd damped it down all those years ago?

'And just what are you plotting now?' Mrs H asked as she watched the many and varied expressions flit across Toby's face. 'You can be just too clever for your own good, you know.'

Giving the housekeeper a startled look, Toby suddenly grinned. 'Didn't fool you for a minute, did I?'

'No,' she said drily. 'Not one.'

Chuckling, Toby finished feeding the baby before giving him his bottle to hold, which he competently put into his mouth, an expression of sheer bliss crossing his chubby face. 'One could almost be forgiven for thinking it was whisky in that instead of milk,' Toby observed.

'Aye, likes his food, doesn't he? So what were you going to tell Marcus? Or were you thinking of adopting the same tactics as with me?'

'Do you think them likely to work?' Toby asked, her face screwed up into a comical grimace.

'No.'

'And you're not going to tell me, either, are you?'

'No.'

'No. That's what I figured. Oh, well, I'll have to think of something else.'

'I don't suppose it occurred to you to just mind your own business? Mrs H asked mildly.

'Well, it did,' Toby confessed, 'but if I've misjudged him, and he's not really a cold, humourless man, or only appears to be because of circumstances, well . . .'

'Well what?' Mrs H asked in astonishment. 'You'll become a kind, understanding companion? Confidante?'

Picturing that very unlikely event, Toby burst out laughing. 'It doesn't seem very likely, does it?'

'No, it doesn't,' Mrs H said, even going so far as to smile. 'Go on, go and put the baby down for his nap. Lunch won't be long and you've got some typing to do, haven't you?'

'Mm. Not so much typing as printing. I'm only half-way through the manual, you see.' Her solemn tones were belied by the twinkle in her eyes. 'I know how to type reports, letters, into memory. I've even discovered how to change the text. What I have not yet discovered is how to get columns of figures lined up on the paper in the exact format the screen shows.'

'Good grief, Toby!' Mrs H exclaimed, for once looking quite shocked. 'Does Marcus know?'

'Er—no,' Toby murmured ruefully. 'So far I've managed to avoid typing financial reports. Oh, well, nothing ventured, nothing gained,' she quipped, her light-hearted tone disguising the fact that she really did want to earn Marcus's praise for efficiency. Not that it was very likely, but it was becoming rather important to her that she shine, that she didn't let him down. She wished there were some magical power that would give her the qualifications she had made up. It had stupidly never occurred to her that she would one day come to regret her hasty actions. Picking the baby up, she took him upstairs for his nap.

The next few days passed swiftly, and if Marcus noticed a new, efficient Toby he didn't mention it.

Neither did he comment on the immaculately typed reports, yet Toby could hardly demand praise when he didn't know she wasn't proficient on the word processor in the first place. She was just beginning to discover the more minor ramifications of telling lies. She was also becoming conscious of the fact that she liked him more than a little, and the point was driven home when he came downstairs, on Thursday evening, resplendent in a dinner suit.

'Don't stare, Toby. It's rude,' he commented mildly, and extending his wrist he added, 'Be a good girl and fix the link for me.'

Girl? she thought as she bent her head to thread the gold link through his shirt-cuff. But I don't want to be a girl. Only, how did you suddenly become a woman in his eyes? Not very easily. And back they were to svelte and sophisicated, she thought with a little smile.

'You look very nice,' she said, standing back to survey him.

'Thank you, Toby,' he said drily. 'Your praise makes me feel so much more confident to face the world.'

'Oh, pooh!' she murmured, poking out her tongue at his sarcasm. As the phone suddenly shrilled, she walked across to answer it. Watching him, she murmured demurely, 'Mr du Mann's residence,' and she saw his lips twitch. No doubt the forthcoming delights of the Savoy and Annabel's had put him in a good humour. She reluctantly dragged her attention back to the phone, and the cool feminine tones. 'Just one moment,' she replied, giving a little scowl at the receiver as she wondered whether the woman on the other end was to be Marcus's companion for the

evening. 'May I ask who's calling? Lydia?' she
practically squealed, her eyes widening. Putting her
hand over the mouthpiece, she stared at Marcus.

No, he mimed, his amusement wiped away as
though it had never been.

'I'm afraid Mr Mann had already left for the
evening,' she said into the phone. 'Yes, I'll tell him.
Goodbye.' Replacing the receiver, 'She said to tell you
she'd called.'

'Thank you, Toby, and you can wipe that look of
speculation off your face.' Straightening the sleeve of
his jacket and brushing at a non-existent speck on the
dark lapel, he added, I'll see you in the morning.
Don't wait up.'

'Oh, humour yet,' she muttered sarcastically as he
turned and walked out. Peeping from the window, she
watched the tail-lights of the Daimler disappear along
the drive.

She only saw him for a few minutes the next morning;
he was up early and already on his way out when she
went downstairs with the baby, so she had no chance
to ask after his evening. It didn't stop her thinking
about it, though. His comings and goings were taking
on far too much importance, she decided crossly, quite
unaware that every time she heard his key in the lock
her face lit up with pleasure. She felt very unsettled all
that day and spent long moments gazing from the
study window at the blue sky. The next day would be
Saturday, and she was hoping that she might get a
chance to use the pool. The weather had been glorious
all week, and it seemed an awful shame to not take
advantage of it. Maybe she'd even get a chance to

teach Peter to swim.

Marcus didn't get home until just before dinner, and then he seemed preoccupied, his answers to her questions, absent, and she wondered if it had anything to do with Lydia. She of the snooty voice on the telephone. She had at least discovered that she was indeed the tall, cool-looking blonde she'd seen in the local shop. She'd also discovered that she wasn't at all popular in the village. Oddly enough, Marcus was, but she guessed that had more to do with the fact that Marcus was one of their own, born and, if not exactly bred in the village, at least his roots had been there. Lydia, on the other hand, was something of an interloper; she had apparently arrived in the village ten years ago, spent only a short time there, before going off to America. So her unpopularity was probably nothing to do with personality although Toby personally thought she didn't have one. In fact she had taken a complete and utter dislike to the other woman. Especially when she discovered Lydia had once been engaged to Marcus. The thought of the elegant blonde crushed in an amorous embrace with her boss didn't sit very well with her at all. Staring at the still face opposite her, she tried to imagine him heartbroken at Lydia's defection when she'd broken off their engagement to marry a wealthy American, and failed. He didn't look as though anything would break his heart. As he looked up suddenly and caught her staring, she queried hastily, 'Bad day?'

'Mm? Oh, no, no more than usual.' Then, putting down his napkin, he asked. 'Excuse me, will you, Toby?' and with a frown that for once wasn't directed at her, he walked out. She heard him run lightly upstairs. Lydia? she wondered. Or some other weighty matter? Lingering over her coffee, her own brow furrowed in thought, she stared absently into the cooling liquid, and it was only the strident ringing on the telephone that prompted her to move. It was Wanda, and Toby spent some moments reassuring her as to Peter's welfare before asking after her husband. When she had put down the phone, she scribbled a note for Marcus to the effect that Anthony was still in intensive care, but stable.

Feeling restless herself, she wandered out into the garden. Walking down to the pool, she stared down into the cold depths, not really seeing the water, but images of Marcus and the lovely, brittle Lydia. Hearing a sound behind her, she turned, and her expression of mild enquiry turned to astonishment. It was Marcus: he'd changed from the elegant suit into a white T-shirt and shorts, his feet encased in trainers, and she found it almost impossible to drag her eyes from the tanned length of strong, muscled legs.

'I do believe I've disconcerted you,' he murmured with a gleam of humour.

'Well, a bit, yes,' she admitted faintly, raising her eyes to his.

'I thought I'd have a knockabout,' he said indicating the tennis court. 'Do you play?'

'What? Oh, yes,' she said quickly, dragging her attention back to his question. Then, a gleam of laughter in her lovely eyes, she murmured. 'And perhaps I should warn you, I'm rather good.' In fact she was more than good. If there was one thing she excelled at, apart from swimming, it was tennis.

She had a natural skill and grace honed almost to perfection by her tennis coach, who had recognised in Toby a supreme talent that was given to very few. It had almost broken his heart when Toby had had to leave school and give it up. It had almost broken hers, too; they'd both visions of a not-so-far-distant Wimbledon.

'Challenging me, Toby?'

'Only at tennis,' she grinned. Turning, she walked away from him toward the court.

As he joined her at the fence surrounding it, he observed quietly, 'It needs resurfacing.' And something in his tone made Toby turn to look at him. His expression was distant, as though he were looking back into a not-too-happy past.

'I expect you used to play a lot,' she proped.

'Mm,' he murmured absently. 'Usually when I was in a temper. A marvellous outlet for anger,' he added, turning to give her a faint smile. 'You can slam the balls around in a fine old display of fury.'

'But not guaranteed to do much for your style,' she said softly, picturing a younger Marcus venting his frustration and temper on the court.

'No,' he said ruefully. Then, putting a companionable arm around her shoulders, her turned her toward the gate in the fence. 'Come along, then, Miss Toby Anderson. Let's see what you're made of.'

Walking across to the little shed, he collected two racquets, then had to struggle to unscrew the press. It had obviously been some time since anyone had used them; the screws looked rusty. Unearthing a couple of balls from the bench drawer, he gave Toby a mocking bow, allowing her to precede him on to the court. 'Do you want to go and change?' he asked rather belatedly.

Glancing down at her full cream skirt, she shook her head. 'I can hitch it up.' This she proceeded to do, turning it over several times at the waistband to expose her strong shapely legs. Kicking off her leather-thonged sandals, she accepted the racquet and balls, a small smile hovering around her mouth. She guessed he thought her earlier words at her prowess were mere bravado. Well he would learn. Tiger Anderson was about to come into her own!

Taking up her position on the base line, and checking to make sure he was ready, she slammed the first ball past him with such speed that he had no chance to react.

'I see,' he murmured wryly. 'Like that, is it?'

Grinning, she moved lithely across to continue her serve and, despite her skirt being hitched rather uncomfortably round her waist, she moved with the fluid grace of the athlete, her gamine face set in lines of concentration. She won the first set, six games to three, and as they changed ends he murmured, 'Can I plead advancing years?'

'Certainly not! For a man in his prime, you're doing very well,' she teased, and was inordinately pleased when he chuckled. Some men she'd played had been furious at being beaten by a woman, and had sulked abominably. Marcus thankfully didn't seem to be one of them. Yet, even if he had, she had no intention of letting him win if she could help it. Although she had to admit that he stretched her to the limit, and on the second set she only won by a small margin. With the late sun beating down on the court creating a heat haze, the game seemed to take on a dreamlike quality. Toby seemed to feel an extra awareness, another dimension to life. The gentle thud of the balls hitting the hard turf, the constantly moving figure of Marcus as he covered the court with long, easy strides. The sound of her breathing, the easy flow of co-ordinated muscles, the sheer enjoyment of doing what she did best. It was a joy, too, to play against someone who could stretch her, make her work, and she was quite unaware that she had a soft smile on her mouth as she ran about the court, or that her husky, infectious laugh rang out more and more frequently. Her hair had given up its fight to stay confined, and curled damply round her laughing face.

At the end of the third set, which they mutually agreed to call a draw when neither could break the other's serve, they walked companionably back to the lawn where Mrs H had delayed her departure to watch the game and set out cold drinks for them.

'Full of surprises, aren't you?' Marcus observed lazily as he lay full length on the grass.

'Only because you'd got it into your head that I was useless,' she murmured, slanting him a wry look. As she passed him a glass of squash, he opened one eye to give her a glance of amusement.

'Where did you learn to play like that?'

'At school. I practise and play whenever I can.' Then, her face taking on a superior expression, she added pompously, 'I'm a memeber at Royal Blackheath.' And when he gave a snort of what could only be called laughter, she grinned.

'I'm surprised they let you,' he murmured, eyeing her crumpled form. She pulled a little face at him, and he asked humorously, 'And what other things aren't you useless at?'

'French,' she murmured. 'Swimming, athletics—and I can half fly a plane!' she added triumphantly.

'Half?' he queried with a grunt of amusement. 'How does one half fly a plane?'

'When one's only had half the lessons, of course. I ran out of money. It's exceedingly expensive to learn to fly, at least forty pounds an hour, and—well, I ran out of money. I'll learn the other half when I'm next in funds.'

Sitting cross-legged, she sipped her own drink and watched him. She'd never seen him so relaxed, so casual, and she smiled, enjoying her appraisal of the strong face and fantastic body. Terrific legs, too.

'Tell me about you,' he demanded softly. 'About your life.'

Leaning back against the table, she transferred her gaze to the garden as she thought over what to tell him. 'I left home when I was eighteen. I was left a small legacy by—a relative,' she murmured. No need to tell him it had been her father, or that her mother insisted she take half of what was left of the insurance money after they'd paid off their debts and go out and enjoy herself. It was ironic, really; when they'd desperately needed money, they had none. The moment he died, they had plenty. Life insurance, she thought with a husky little laugh, but only when life was gone, and her eyes for a moment were sad. 'I bummed around Europe for two years, that's how I learned French, or at least how I learned to speak it fluently. I shared a flat with a French girl for a while. It was her boyfriend who taught me to fly. When I ran out of funds, I came back to England. Went to stay with Mum for a bit, just drifting.' And she'd been drifting ever since, she suddenly realised. One job after another. One town after another, dreary bedsits, cheap hotels, never staying anywhere too long, never becoming serious. Yet it had been during this period that a chance remark about her prowess in the water had prompted her to train as a swimming instructor. She'd discovered it was possible to enrol for evening tuition at Crystal Palace to take her ASA Preliminary, then the ASA Teacher's Certificate, and then the Advanced course if she wanted to work in London. Much to everyone's surprise she had taken it far more seriously than anyone expected. Certainly she had never regretted the six months it had taken to train. She'd found a tempory job as a copy typist to pay for the course and the cost of her accommodation in a small lodging house, and to her great delight she had passed all three courses with distinction.

'And?' he prompted. 'No romances along the way? No undying passion, Toby?'

'No. No undying passion.' she murmured. Because I'm an emotional coward. Because I won't let love grow. Because love can destroy you. It had almost destroyed her mother.

Giving him a brief smile, she turned to stare toward, the house. She didn't want to talk about herself any more. It only emphasised the shallowness of her existence. Being a court jester was sometimes very tiring.

The late sun gave the house a golden glow, mellowed the old stone, and it didn't look at all the sort of house one would hate. 'It's been in your family a long time, hasn't it?' she said softly, needing to change the subject because she knew he watched her, speculated, and she cursed herself for revealing more of herself than she had intended. It was best he saw her as a ninny. Best she played the game to its final conclusion—whatever that might be. Turning to glance at him, she prompted, 'How long?'

'Too long.' Giving a sigh, he leaned up on one elbow to follow her glance toward the house. 'An ugly brick edifice that my sister laughingly calls home,' he muttered broodingly, his mood changing.

'You hate it, don't you?' she asked softly.

'Yes, Toby, I hate it. It seems to echo with the unhappy ghosts of past du Manns.'

'They weren't all unhappy, surely?'

'Probably not,' he said moodily. 'It just seems that way.'

'Because you were unhappy here?' And she wasn't really surprised at the harsh laugh he gave.

'Probably. There was never any peace, no quiet moments. It was a permanent battleground. Whatever I did, whatever I wanted, whatever I was, was wrong. Father and son, cleaved from the same stone, moulded from the same clay. There should have been a bond, an understanding, but there was only hatred.'

'Yet he left you the house,' she said, perplexed. If his father had hated him so much, why leave him the house and his money?

'He had no choice. It was entailed,' he explained.

'He wanted it to go to Wanda? Is that why you allow her to live here?'

'It was no good to me,' he said indifferently, 'and she loved it.'

'And her father? Is that why you looked startled

when she threw herself into your arms when we first came? Because you'd never been close?'

'Mm. My fault, probably,' he murmured. 'Displays of affection between us were, to say the least, rare.'

'But you didn't hate her?'

'Hate her?' he asked astonished. 'Why on earth should I hate her?'

'Well, because your father loved her and not you, because her life here was so different to yours.' An echo of Mrs H's words in her head, that she was the old man's darling. When he didn't answer, she turned to look at him, then gave a shamefaced grin at his wry look.

'Who told you that?'

'Oh—er—I heard it in the village, I think,' she invented hastily.

'What else did you just—er—hear?'

'I wasn't gossiping about you, Marcus!' she defended quickly. 'You know how it is, people take an interest in everyone else and . . .'

'Regale newcomers will all sorts of gossip? That naturally you didn't know, but were too polite to ignore?'

'Yes.'

'So what else did they just tell you? Mm?'

'Only about Lydia,' she murmured huskily, giving him a wary look.'

'My, my, you *have* been busy,' he said with an edge of sarcasm.

'Oh, Marcus, come on. It wasn't meant maliciously. I won't pretend I wasn't interested, because I was. But not to be nosy or anything.'

'What other reasons are there, Toby? Avid curiosity is being nosy.'

'No, it isn't!' she exclaimed, swivelling round to face him. 'Not in the way you mean. I just thought that maybe if I'd misjudged you, and that you weren't . . .' She tailed lamely off as she realised that she could hardly tell him what she had thought, especially in the face of his scepticism.

'Autocratic? Bad-tempered? Despotic?' he asked helpfully, with an ironioc lift of one eyebrow.

'Well, something like that,' she muttered. 'I mean, if you had a horrendous childhood and everything, and then Lydia jilting you, then coming back to upset you all over again . . .'

'My God!' he exclaimed. 'You don't pull your punches, do you?'

'Oh,' she murmured guiltily, 'is it a taboo subject? I mean, it was ten years ago, and well . . . Did you love her very much?' she asked softly. 'Because really, you know, I didn't think her at all the sort to generate undying devotion. I found her . . .'

'One of these days, Miss Anderson,' he broke in, 'Someone is going to bop you on the nose. And at the rate you're going, it might very well be me!'

As he got to his feet, she said worriedly, 'It's only because I like you.'

'Like me?' he exclaimed in astonishment. 'I dread to think what you'd do if you hated me!' And, giving a rueful shake of his head, he walked quickly toward the house.

'Oh, bumblies!' she muttered. That wasn't very clever, Toby. Collecting up the glasses, she went inside to shower and change. When she came down, Marcus called her into the study and she wondered if she was to get a little homily on minding her own business. However, the incident in the garden wasn't mentioned, it was for a quite different reason that he wanted her.

'You don't need to look as though you're going to the Tower. I merely wanted to pay you,' he said drily. He took an envelope from the top drawer of his desk and tossed it casually across to her.

Giving him a little grin, she picked it up, then stared in astonishment at the amount written on the front. It was for twenty pounds more then she was expecting. Lifting her eyes awkwardly to his, she explained, 'You've paid me too much,' a statement which seemed to startle him far more than her mild words warranted.

'You wanted extra for looking after the baby, didn't you? Well, now you're got extra.'

'Extra? I didn't ask for extra,' she said slowly, her own brows drawn into a frown.

'Oh, for goodness' sake,' he said, exasperated. 'We were sitting at the kitchen table!'

'But I didn't say I wanted extra. I asked if I was getting the same, and you told me I had a pre-occupation with money that bordered on the unhealthy.'

'Well?' he said impatiently.

'Well, I meant, were you going to pay me less? I can't take extra, Marcus,' she began worriedly. It was bad enough having lied about her qualifications, without taking extra money from him. He could hardly put looking after his sister's baby as a justifiable expense, which meant it must have come from his own pocket.

'Really, I can't,' she repeated when he only continued to look dumbfounded. Taking twenty pounds from the envelope, she put it on the desk in front of him.

'I don't understand you,' he murmured faintly, pushing the money back toward her. 'I really don't.' When she didn't pick it up he did it for her, and, getting to his feet and walking round the desk, he pushed it into her hand. 'Keep it. And don't argue, Toby,' he muttered as she opened her mouth. 'Just don't argue.' With a puzzled shake of his head, he went out. Staring worriedly after him, she finally pushed the money back into the envelope. Perhaps she could buy him something with it, or the baby, because she really couldn't keep it for herself. It wasn't the fact of the money that troubled her, but that she had got it under false pretences. Probably twenty pounds was nothing to him, but it was the principle of the thing. It was all very difficult. It had all seemed so simple at the interview.

It didn't seem any simpler the next morning. Marcus was nowhere in evidence, and the house felt empty, abandoned. She missed him, and that would be clever, wouldn't it? To like him too much. That would be poetic justice with a vengeance. Here he was, this attractive man. Too attractive. In good employment, wealthy, in fact. Perfect in every way—fitting her nebulous criteria exactly. Except that her thoughts and ideas had not incorporated feelings. Not strong feelings, anyway. It had been a Alice in Wonderland vision, without depth. Strong feelings, as she knew to her cost, made you vulnerable, open to hurt. So, there must be none. They must be squashed very firmly at birth. Apart from which, the odds on him reciprocating any feelings she might have were absolutely nil. So put your thoughts away, Toby Anderson. Put them away. Which, because it was what she'd always done, she assumed would be easy. Or, if not easy, then possible.

With the morning stretching emptily before her, she decided to expend some of her restless energy by teaching Peter to swim. She only kept him in the water for half an hour, which she thought quite long enough for his first lesson. Not that he agreed; as soon as she took him out, he began howling and it took her some time to soothe him, which wasn't like him at all. She hoped he wasn't sickening for something. He was usually very sunny-natured.

As soon as she returned to the house, the phone rang. Lydia. Not once, but half a dozen times, until Toby became thoroughly exasperated.

'He's not here!' she snapped. 'No, I do not know where he is—yes, I will tell him you called—no, I haven't forgotten.' Rolling her eyes upward, she pulled horrible faces at the phone. Dratted woman. 'Lydia,' she broke in, 'I'm not an answering machine! I've told you I'll tell him, and I will!' Slamming the phone down, she shook her head. Stupid woman. She didn't know why Marcus didn't just tell her to get lost. Because, if he didn't, she was more than tempted to. She was beginning to dislike her intensely.

When he did return, at just gone seven, Toby was half-heartedly practising the guitar.

'Hi,' she said easily after a very thorough appraisal of his person. She felt as though she hadn't seen him for years, then smiled when he gave her a suspicious look. 'Have you eaten?' she asked kindly.

'Yes, Miss Anderson, I have eaten,' he said sardonically, 'and if you ask me where I've been, I shall probably become violent. Why the spurious concern, anyway?'

'Oh, no reason,' she said airily. 'And you shouldn't grind your teeth,' she added mildly, stretching her fingers to find the G chord. 'It's very bad for your jaw.' And just what had put him in a bad mood? she wondered. When he didn't answer, she flicked him a glance from under her lashes. Laying her guitar on her knees, she said flatly, 'Lydia phoned, and phoned.' And when he only gave her a look of sorely tried patience, she added waspishly, 'You shouldn't let her get away with it, you know,' then gave a funny little grimace as he threw himself into the chair opposite in a gesture of defeat. The folder of papers he'd been carrying he threw down on the floor.

'Miss Anderson, I have a report I need to digest before an important meeting on Monday.'

'Well, you won't take it in if your mind's on something else, will you? It's no good pushing things to the back of your mind, hoping they'll go away. You have to stop Lydia now, otherwise she'll have you down the aisle before you know what's hit you.'

'Do you really think so?' he queried flatly, his eyes hard on hers. 'Do I really look the sort of man to be led by the nose? Or incapable of sorting out my own affairs?'

'No-o, not normally, no. But women like Lydia can be very devious, and I don't think you quite realise the lengths to which she will go.'

'Not only Lydia,' he muttered, bending to retrieve

his papers.

'Don't be pompous. And it's no good being complacent. She wants you back,' Toby stated bluntly.

'Rubbish!'

'Not so. It's all round the village . . .'

'Oh, is it?' he said grimly, and Toby belatedly realised that that possibly hadn't been quite the best way to go about things. 'And who put it about the village, Miss Anderson?'

'Well, not me!' she exclaimed hastily, giving him a look of injured innocence.

'Were you born with this insatiable curiosity about other people's affairs? Or is it a talent only lately realised?' he asked with oily sarcasm.

'Don't be poky, Marcus. I'm only trying to help.'

'Kind of you.'

'Because,' she continued forcefully, 'I cannot by any stretch of the imagination possibly conceive of one reason why you would be so lacking in perception as to let her get her red little claws into you, but seeing as you obviously are, I've decided to help. So, we must devise a plan.'

'No, Miss Anderson,' he corrected, 'we must not devise a plan. We must mind our own business.'

'Do you want to get back together?' she asked incredulously. 'I mean, I suppose if you're still in love with her . . .'

'No, I am not still in love with her!' he gritted. 'And we are not back together!'

'Well, *I* know that, and *you* know that, but does anyone else?' she asked.

'Miss Anderson . . .' he began wearily.

'Toby,' she corrected. 'Why don't you call me Toby? You did before.'

'Because I don't want to call you Toby. I don't want to call you anything at all, and if it wasn't for the fact that I need you to look after my nephew, you'd be out of this house so fast your feet wouldn't touch the ground!'

'Would I? Yes, I suppose I would,' she admitted honestly, and wouldn't analyse the awful feeling of emptiness that came over her. Just because they'd seemed to be getting on, didn't necessarily mean he would ever like her. She'd been in danger of forgetting that. Swallowing the hurt his words caused, unaware that her lovely eyes reflected her confusion, she battled on, 'But I really would like to help.'

'Why?'

'Well, because you need it,' she said, not quite truthfully, and at his look of scepticism she added more honestly, 'And because I don't like her. She didn't like me very much, either,' she admitted.

'Not surprising,' he muttered. 'Do I even dare ask where you met?'

'Oh, we haven't met,' she confessed. 'We've only spoken on the phone.' Marcus gave her a look of impatience, and she added crossly, 'I don't need to meet her to know I don't like her! She seems to think she can pick up where she left off,' she muttered, incensed all over again by Lydia's arrogance. 'And she will if you're not careful,' she warned.

'And you arrogantly assume that you are the very person to solve this dilemma?' he asked cynically. 'Very generous of you, I'm sure, and you have also no doubt worked out the very way to do it?'

'Well, yes, sort of. If you won't tell her to get lost, then you could pretend to be in love with me.'

'Oh surprise, surprise,' he said sarcastically, giving her a look of disgust before returning his attention to his report.

'Well, there's no need to be so rude, I only said *pretend,*' she reproved, although it was really only what she might expected. 'I was only trying to help.'

'No, you weren't, Miss Anderson, you were trying to further your own cause. And do you genuinely think anyone would believe I had fallen madly in love with you?' he asked disparagingly, looking up for a moment to eye her rumpled form, his eyes lingering on the wisps of hair that had again escaped confinement.

'Not madly, no,' she grinned, 'but stranger things have happened.'

'Not to me they haven't,' he said dismissively.

Despite the disparagement in his tone, his words made Toby laugh. 'And what do you mean *further my own cause?*' she asked. 'I don't have a cause. I just thought you deserved better than Lydia.'

'Really?' he asked, disbelief written all over him.

'Yes, really.' She didn't want him to fall in love with her. Of course she didn't. She just liked him, that was all. Leaning back in her chair, she watched him. The long, elegant fingers that held the pen too tight as he scored through the report. Not hers, thank goodness. The concentration that firmed this features and those bright eyes that came as such as shock when he flicked her an irritated glance. The thick, dark hair had a sprinkling of grey at the temples, she suddenly noticed. A complete person. Immaculate. And, no matter how hard she tried, she usually looked as though she'd been pulled through several hedges backwards, which made it seem even more unlikely that anyone would believe he was in love with her. Or even *like* her, come to that. Only it didn't have to be believed, only act as a red herring, and no one was likely to accuse him of lying. If he said he was in love with her, unlikely as it might seem, they had to at least consider the possibility.

Was he a good lover? she wondered involuntarily. 'Are you a good lover?' she murmured, without any idea that she was about to say anything so stupid. 'Sorry,' she muttered, pulling a face. 'I didn't mean to say that.'

'Oh, for God's sake!' he exploded, tossing the report back on to the floor. 'Will you go away? Go to bed or something!'

'It's only eight o'clock,' she pointed out, glancing at the clock, 'and it's cold in my bedroom.'

'Well, if that's an invitation to join me in mine, forget it!'

Staring at him in astonishment, she suddenly burst out laughing, which seemed to surprise him. 'I don't want to join you in your bed! Heaven forbid! I'd never cope with someone like you. I'm not in the least experienced, you know.' Yet she felt an awful warmth steal over her as an image of him making love to her grew rather too graphically in her mind.

'Don't tell me you're a virgin. That I won't believe!'

'I didn't say I was a virgin, only that I wasn't experienced. Certainly not experienced enough to know what to do with someone like you.'

'What in God's name do you imagine I do?' he

asked in astonishment.

'Well, I don't know—*things*,' she murmured vaguely. 'I expect you have sophisticated tastes.' She'd never actually thought about it before, but he lived in such a totally different world from her own, that he was bound to do things differently. Wasn't he?

'Bondage? Whips?' he asked with mild sarcasm.

'No! Well, at least, that wasn't what I had in mind,' she murmured, only the sudden mental image she had of him in black leather with a whip in one hand made her give a gurgle of involuntary laughter.

'Then what did you have in mind? I'd very much like to know what that fertile little brain of yours imagines I do that others don't.'

'Well, I don't know. Not precisely, I just thought it probably wasn't the same as—well, what I'd do.' Oh, hell, now look where her big mouth had got her. She'd meant to tease him, and now they were heavily into fetish. Good lord, Toby, why don't you learn to behave? There was also dangerous excitement threading along her nerves, and she knew full well she should abandon her teasing. Only she stupidly didn't want to.

'Then what precisely, Miss Anderson, do you do?' he asked silkily, getting to his feet, a rather ominous look on his face, 'Or perhaps bondage is more in your line?'

'Don't be silly,' she mumbled, then hastily vacated her chair and scrambled behind it as he advanced rather menacingly toward her. 'Marcus?' she squealed in alarm.

'You want to play games, Miss Anderson? Very well, then we'll play games.'

Staring at him in horror, she wondered how on earth everything had suddenly got so out of hand. He didn't at all look as though he were teasing. A strategic retreat seemed in order. As she went to dash past him, he grabbed her arm and hauled her round before slamming her none too gently against the wall. He then fitted one large hand round her neck. Surely he wasn't going to strangle her? Yet the tension in him was like a palpable aura, and she felt a swift stab of fear. Her heart was racing far too fast, and God only knew what had happened to her breathing as she stared into hard blue eyes that were far too close to her own.

'Big, innocent eyes,' he said softly. 'Come-to-bed eyes. To look at you, Miss Anderson, one would never guess at the plotting and planning that goes on behind that gentle façade. At the ruthless pursuit of goals . . .'

'What goals?' she croaked huskily. The only goals she had were to pay her rent and decimate the lovely Lydia. That wasn't so terrible, was it? 'You seem to have some very odd ideas about me,' she added breathlessly.

'Do I?' he asked with suspect mildness. 'Now, I wonder why? You see, Miss Anderson, I have this odd idea—ridiculous, I'm sure—that I'm being manipulated, manoeuvred. Now isn't that an odd notion? Nothing to say? No? And we never did conclude the riddle of how you got an O-level in domestic science when you can't cook, did we?'

'No,' she whispered, beginning to feel almost mesmerised by those bright blue eyes. There was no expression in their depths, no humour, just bright blue, the pupil large and black, accusing, which made it very difficult to think.

'So why was that, Miss Anderson?'

'I don't know,' she mumbled huskily, glancing frantically to left and right for an avenue of escape.

'Expecting someone?' he asked softly.

'No. Oh, no,' she said hastily. 'Just wondered if I ought to pray for divine intervention,' she murmured with an attempt at humour that fell sadly flat.

'Why? You're in my arms, my mouth is only inches away from yours. You have the perfect opportunity to find out what sort of lover I am. Don't you?'

'I don't want to make love to you!' she gasped, horrified. 'I was teasing! You know I was!' Trust him to get the wrong end of the stick. Yet her heart had given the most awful lurch at his words—but she didn't, did she? Determined to negate the thought, she said forcefully, 'I don't! And you certainly don't want to make love to me.'

'Oh, I don't know,' he drawled. 'You have a certain gamine charm. You're no beauty, I grant you, but not exactly an antidote. I'm quite willing to oblige you,' he said silkily.

'Well, I don't want you to oblige me! Stop playing games, Marcus!'

'To quote you,' he drawled, 'I wasn't aware that I was.' Then, without warning, he moved his hand beneath her shirt to cup her breast, which made Toby gasp with shock and belatedly begin to struggle.

'You just dare,' she gritted, then could have laughed hysterically, because he just had. 'I'm warning you, Marcus! I'll . . .'

'What?' he murmured, then effectively shut her up by kissing her. And Toby went rigid with shock, because the feel of that warm mouth on hers turned her whole emotionally well-ordered life upside-down. It tossed out all preconceived notions of choice. And it terrified the life out of her.

It wasn't a gentle, exploratory kiss, and the feelings he generated were feelings she'd never felt before. Never dreamed existed . . . And now she was learning first-hand just how wrong she had been. About everything.

CHAPTER FIVE

IN TOTAL panic Toby lashed out at him, and only succeeded in hurting her hand. Clenching her fingers in his hair, she yanked hard, and when his mouth left hers she dragged in a sobbing breath. 'Take your hands off me,' she said hoarsely.

His eyes holding hers, Marcus moved his hands and leaned them flat on the wall either side of her head. His face was still, the eyes hard.

'I don't want this, Marcus,' she said raggedly. 'I don't.'

'Liar.'

'I'm not lying!' she yelled, shoving his arm away. 'I'm not!' Ducking past him, she ran. Pounding up the stairs as though the devil himself were on her heels, she didn't stop until she was safely in her room. 'I'm not,' she whispered to herself. Dragging in a deep, shuddering breath, she closed her eyes tight for a moment, only to whirl in alarm as the door opened behind her. 'No,' she breathed, her eyes wide and frightened as he leaned in the doorway. As she read the purpose in those blue eyes she burst out, 'Stop it! Stop looking at me like that!'

'How am I looking?'

'Like a hungry cat that's just found a juicy mouse to torment!'

'Ah.' Then, with slow deliberation, he began walking across the room toward her.

'Marcus, no!' she yelled, scrambling hastily across the bed to the other side. 'Stop being ridiculous! I was only teasing, you know I was!'

'Do I?' he asked softly, advancing round the end of the bed until Toby was pressed up in the corner beside the wardrobe with nowhere left to go.

'Yes, you damn well do! Stop being provocative. It's very late, Marcus. I want to go to bed. We can discuss it in the morning.'

'Very well,' he capitulated, causing Toby to blink at him in astonishment, and then, to her horror, he wrenched off his tie and began unbuttoning his shirt.

'What are you doing?' she gasped.

'Why, getting ready for bed,' he said, as though it were the most natural thing in the world and he was astonished at her lack of understanding.

'Not here!'

'But of course here.' And, with a rather evil smile pulling at his mouth, he glanced casually toward the bed.

'This is not funny, Marcus,' she gritted.

'No,' he agreed, and the way he said it, with a rather menacing undertone, made Toby close her eyes momentarily in defeat. She felt a hysterical desire to scream, and go on screaming.

'Oh, God,' she whispered weakly. How on earth had she got herself into such a mess? 'No!' she yelled as she felt his hand begin on the buttons of her shirt. 'Oh, no!' Clamping her own hands round his in a futile effort to prevent him, she added sternly, 'For God's sake, Marcus, enough's enough! What the hell do you think you're doing?'

'Undressing you,' he said mildly. 'You can't go to bed fully dressed, now can you? It takes all the fun out of it.'

'Marcus, you undo one more button, and I'll—I'll knee you!' Really, it was so utterly ridiculous, he was behaving totally out of character. She couldn't believe he would go through with it. He'd known she was teasing!

'But you want me—you said so——'

'I didn't!' she yelled.

' . . . and I want, *need*, satisfying. After all, you've chased away the only other candidate,' he taunted softly.

'Marcus, please don't,' she begged, hating herself for sounding so breathless as his fingers easily disengaged hers. Before she knew quite what he was about, she had both her hands trapped behind her in one of his while the other dealt easily with her buttons.

'No! No, oh, no, Marcus, please. You have no more desire to make love to me than I have to you. You know you don't!' His fingers were warm against her flesh and her breath was coming in jerky little rushes. 'Oh, please,' she gasped, trying futilely to wrench her wrists from his grasp. 'Stop playing games and go away!' And the scorn she was trying to inject into her voice just wasn't there, she noted with despair. She just couldn't believe it had all got so out of hand.

'But I like silly games—they're my absolute favourite.'

'They are *not* your absolute favourite!' she hissed. She finally admitted to herself that he wasn't joking at all but was in deadly earnest. 'All right, all right,' she yelped. 'I'm sorry. I won't do it again. In future I will be a model of . . . Marcus!' she protested hoarsely, as he leaned his hips against hers, terrifying the life out of her. 'Please don't do this,' she whispered, her lovely eyes fixed widely on his in mute plea. 'No!' she screamed as he picked her up and lay her on the bed, his own warm, hard body covering hers. She lay very, very still as powerful thighs touched against her own. His breath was warm on her parted mouth, and she was terrified of saying or doing the wrong thing in case she precipitated the very thing she was desperately trying to avoid.

'Not even tempted, Toby?' he whispered softly, his eyes trapping hers in their bright blue depths.

'No,' she croaked. Which was a complete and utter lie. She was tempted, terribly tempted, and she found she had to hold her breath, lock it in her lungs in an effort to negate the thoughts racing rather erotically round her head.

'Don't want to run your palms down my back?' She shook her head in strenuous denial. 'Touch me?'

'No.' It was extraordinarily difficult to force the words from her dry throat. The feeling of his warm flesh on hers was setting up all sorts of alarming sensations in the pit of her stomach. His eyes were mesmerising her, hypnotic. She could feel her traitorous body relaxing and there was a terrible temptation to say yes. To give in. He was wildly attractive, and strong, and she liked him. And she wished she could faint. 'It will be rape,' she breathed, staring widely at him. 'It will, Marcus.'

'No, Toby. It won't,' he said with soft menace—and she knew it wouldn't. Knew without a shadow of doubt that she would respond—and that terrified her more than anything else. With a surge of strength that she hadn't know herself capable of, she heaved upwards and scrambled hastily away. Half falling to the floor, she felt her ankle gripped and she fell heavily. Lashing out, she caught him a blow on the side of the head—and then he was no longer half teasing as he had been before. Now he was in deadly earnest as he lost his temper.

Dragging her round so that she was pressed painfully against the side of the bed, he stared grimly into her frightened face. 'I'm not a silly boy to be teased and manoeuvred,' he grated. 'You should have remembered that! Little girls who play with fire should expect to be burned.'

To her infinite and everlasting relief, Peter woke up. For a moment Marcus looked as though he hated her. Really hated her. His mouth took on a bitter twist, and he dragged a deep breath into his lungs before throwing her hands away from him. 'See to the baby! And perhaps that will be a lesson to you not to play stupid, childish games. Games, like lies, can get totally out of control.' Then, with a swift movement that took her by surprise, he got to his feet, collected up his clothes and stalked out.

Toby was shaking almost uncontrollably and her breath came in harsh gasps as she lay sprawled untidily across the edge of the bed where he had left her. Her hair was a wild tangle round her white face, her eyes wide with shock, and she felt sick. She'd wanted him. Wanted him to touch her, make love to her, and she shook her head again, as though the action might deny the facts. Her hand still burned where she had touched him. 'No,' she whispered. 'Oh, no.'

As the baby gave another cry, she sprang to her feet and ran into the nursery, glad to action, any action to push the feel of Marcus from her mind. Picking him up, she held the warm body to her.

'It's all right, Toby's here,' she whispered, but the warmth of his body only brought back the warmth of another as her mind played the scene in the bedroom over and over again. 'No,' she kept whispering. 'No.' No, she thought, almost fiercely. She would not let herself care, or feel. That way lay heartbreak. Never, never, she thought vehemently, would she be caught in that trap. As she absently soothed the baby, walking backwards and forwards, it only gradually dawned on her that he was very hot. His little face was burning up. 'Oh, God, please don't let him be ill,' she prayed. Perhaps if she changed him, he *was* very wet, gave him a cool drink, he would be all right, go back to sleep. Only he didn't. It was more grizzling than loud cries, but he was obviously in pain, and she hadn't a clue what to do. As Marcus walked in, clad now in his navy robe, she turned to him almsot gratefully.

'What's wrong with him?' he asked, sounding as worried as she felt.

'I don't know,' she whispered, her voice wobbling uncertainly. 'I don't know anything about babies. I told you I didn't.' And her voice rose shrilly for a second before she managed tok get it under control. 'Sorry. Panic,' she explained, a pleading expression in her lovely eyes.

'What about an aspirin or something?' he asked hopefully, and it would have been comical if she hadn't been so desperately worried. 'God, he's burning up,' he muttered coming over to put a hand on the baby's forehead.

'I know. Oh, Marcus . . .'

'Now, don't panic, Toby,' he said sternly, sounding as though he was going to be just that himself. 'It's probably quite simple. Where's Wanda's list?'

'In the kitchen.'

'Right.'

Toby stared after him in astonishmnent as he disappeared out the door. She could feel a little bubble of hysteria welling up, and she clamped down hard on her bottom lip. If anyone was going to fall apart, she wanted it to be her. Not him! Why couldn't men cope with illness, she thought, totally unfairly. Yet they never seemed to—did they? Her married friends always seemed to say, 'Oh, him, he's useless'. She didn't want him to be useless, she wanted him to cope. Despite what had happened betwen them, she needed him, needed his solid strength. She'd never cope on her own.

'Doesn't tell us very much, does it?' he asked, quickly scanning the instructions as he walked back in. Then, as Peter rammed his fist into his mouth, worrying it back back and forth, their eyes met over the baby's head.

'Teething,' they said together, then both laughed in relief.

Letting her breath out on a long sigh, she smiled at him. 'Sorry,' she apologised, 'I should have realised earlier.'

'Why?' he asked softly. 'Don't have a degree in it, do you?' And, as she shook her head, he added almost huskily, 'Hadn't you better put your robe on? You might—er—catch cold.' He walked rather quickly into the bathroom to investigate the contents of the medicine cabinet. A wave of embarrassment washing over her, Toby scurried into her room to grab her robe; in the worry over the baby she'd completely forgotten that she was still only clad in bra and pants. Trying to struggle into it and hold the baby at the same time, she felt rather than heard Marcus come up behind her.

'Here,' he said softly, and, putting out rather hesitant hands, a comical grimace on his face, he gingerly took the baby then walked back into the nursery as though he were carrying eggs. But at least her slight amusement at his behaviour served to take away the awful dryness she'd felt in her throat when he'd glanced at her. Taking a deep breath, she hastily shrugged into the soft silk before knotting it firmly round her.

Her legs felt decidely wobbly, she decided as she walked back to the nusery, and, avoiding Marcus's eyes, she sank gratefully into the nursing chair. Taking the baby from him, she rocked him gently back and forwards. Murmuring little words to him, as comfort for both of them, she thought ruefully, she glanced up as Marcus came to stand in front of her, a small tube in his hand.

'I think you rub it on his gums,' he murmured, peering intently at the label. Squeezing a small amount on to his little finger, giving her a warm smile as he did so, he teased, 'They are clean, I just washed them.'

'I wasn't criticising,' she said softly.

'I know.'

Turning Peter round, she held his head steady as

Marcus gently rubbed cream on to his gums, then settled him back against her, his hot face pressed into her neck.

'Lucky baby,' Marcus murmured rather thickly, and as Toby looked at him startled he grinned. 'I've got bruises.'

Flushing, she rested her face on the baby's soft hair, unable to look at him. Unable, as he had been to make light of it.

'At least he's stopped crying,' she murmured throatily, 'I don't know how mothers can bear it when babies cry. It really screwed me up,' she muttered, desperately needing to change the subject. 'I'll stay with him a while, till he goes to sleep.'

'Want anything?' he asked gently, as though understanding her reluctance to discuss their earlier behaviour. 'Tea? Coffee?'

'Tea, please.' She'd been grateful earlier for his presence, now she was grateful that he'd gone. Keep it light, she adjured herself. Must keep it light. Only she knew it was far, far too late. Leaning back in the chair, she stared through the window at the moon, not really seeing it, not seeing anything except Marcus's face just before he'd left. The hatred and bitterness that had stamped his features earlier had completely gone. His temper had evaporated. Yet he'd been so angry before. Why? Because, against his will, he'd felt something? Desire, need, want. Something. Was that it? Did he hate himself for becoming aroused? Aroused by a woman he disliked? No, don't think about why, Toby. It doesn't matter why. Childish, he'd called her—and childish she must remain, because she couldn't cope with anything else. She really couldn't.

Only, how to banish the feelings? How to banish that want?

Giving a long, shaky sigh, she dropped a light kiss on Peter's head. In some ways, she was as much a child as he. But deliberately so. The emotion of loving had nearly destroyed her mother, her father's bitterness and railing against fate had tested it to the limit, and Toby had sworn that she would never put herself in that postion. She would live life on the surface, be independent, pay her own way, and if she ever met anyone she thought she could be happy with, provided he was well established, then that would be fine.

Had she really been so childish as to believe that? she wondered. Could she really have been such a fool? You live a lie, Toby Anderson, and now you're so enmeshed in it that you don't know who you are any more. You cover up your feelings with jokes and lighthearted behaviour, and now it's such an intergral part of your character that you don't know any other to behave. What sort of person would she have been if her father hadn't had his accident? Hadn't died? There was no way of knowing.

As Marcus returned, carrying two mugs, she turned her head to give him a lame smile. 'Thank you,' she murmured rather huskily as he put the mug beside her on the cabinet. It was no wonder he got exasperated with her, her behaviour to date would have been enough to try a saint. 'Marcus?'

'Mm?' he murmured softly, perching on the window-seat, his mug between his palms.

'I'm sorry. I've been an awful pain, haven't I?'

'Oh, shocking,' he teased. 'Been doing a bit of soul searching, Toby?' he asked, so kindly that her eyes filled with silly tears.

'Something like that, she murmured huskily.

'Mm. People often do between midnight and dawn. By tomorrow I expect you'll be back to your usual impossible self.' But the words weren't said nastily. He'd sounded almost amused. Then, peering over her shoulder, he added, 'I think he's gone to sleep.'

'Yes. I'll wait a few moments to be sure, then I'll put him down. Why don't you go and get some sleep? It seems silly, both of us staying up.' His presence now was no longer a pleasure, but a pain. There was the most awful ache in her chest, a prickling behind her eyes, and she thought she wanted to weep. But not in front of Marcus.

As he nodded and got to his feet, Toby avoided his eyes, only relaxing as the door closed behind him.

Not surprisingly, she didn't sleep very well, and the lies she'd told seemed to hang ominously over her head like the sword of Damocles. He'll find out, Sally had said. Doesn't seem the sort of man to be amused. No, he definitely wouldn't be amused. It might be wise to tell him now, before he found out from, somewhere else. In fact, she *wanted* to tell him now. Wanted there to be honesty between them.

Hearing gurgled murmurs from the nursery, she reluctantly got out of bed. She felt totally unrefreshed, and for the first time since she'd met him she felt a reluctance to face Marcus. Had he slept? There was no reason why not. His conscience was clear.

Walking through into the nursery, she smiled as chubby arms went out in greeting. 'Hello, back to normal?' she asked softly. Picking him up, hugging the warm body to her, she murmured, 'I'm going to miss you, aren't I?' It was almost a week since Wanda had gone, and yet sometimes it seemed like she had been living this life for ever. It wouldn't be easy to readjust, she thought. Despite Marcus and the way he made her feel, she found she didnt want to leave, not really. But then, she didn't think she could bear to stay. But she would tell him the truth, and today.

She'd already put Peter out in his pram, when Marcus came down, and Toby eyed him warily. She wished he had bothered to dress first, as she had; the thought of that naked body beneath the navy towelling robe was doing peculiar things to her breathing.

With an amused lift of one eyebrow, he asked, 'Baby all right?'

'Yes, he seems fine.' She couldn't think of anything else to say. He didn't look as though he'd spent a sleepless night, she thought resentfully.

Mrs H didn't come in on Sundays, and she asked, rather hesitantly. 'Do you want some breakfast?'

'Practising your domesticity, Toby?' he asked smoothly.

'No, I am not!' she said, exasperated, her awareness of him finding outlet in a burst of temper. 'Why can't you just answer yes or no for a change?' When his only answer was to raise one eyebrow, she became thoroughly infuriated. 'Well, do you?' she demanded.

'No, thank you. Just tea will do,' he murmured, sounding for all the world as though he was trying not to laugh. 'I'll have something later.'

Fetching him a cup, she plonked it in front of him. Resuming her own seat, she gripped her cup hard. She felt thoroughly unsettled and quite unlike her normal self. And for that, she thought, she could hate him. No man had ever made her feel so self-conscious and awkward, and she resented it. Or she tried to, because that was safer. She still had a few days to get through yet, but it was desperately hard. He kept staring at her, too, and when she was unable to stand it any longer she got awkwardly to her feet. Taking her cup across to the sink, she asked, 'Do you need me to work today?'

'No, Miss Anderson,' he murmured blandly, 'I do not need you to work today. You may spend it how you choose.'

'Thank you,' she mumbled grumpily, and, slamming down her washed cup, stalked out into the garden. Staring at the grounds, her mind in turmoil, she only gradually registered how inviting the pool looked. She'd swim, that was what she'd do. But later, when the sun had had a chance to warm the water. First she'd push the pram down to the village, get a paper—that would pass some time, and hopefully by then he'd have dressed. Never in her life had she ever had to invent things to do. Sundays in her flat were taken up with various projects, even if it was only cleaning. Ironically, she'd often longed just to be lazy, lie around with nothing much to do, yet now she had the opportunity she found herself unable to take advantage of the fact.

Collecting some change from her room, ignoring Marcus, who was still at the kitchen table, she walked down to the village. The sun was warm on her back and Toby gradually relaxed. She could cope with her feelings, she decided. She'd have to. If they weren't nurtured, like a plant, they would die. And she very firmly squashed the little thought that they'd no such thing.

It was only as she walked to the house that she registered the total peace. Even the muted tolling of the church bell hardly disturbed the air. It was as though she was the only person in the world. Even the birds seemed silent. God in his heaven and all right with the world. She wished.

Her feelings of abandonment seemed to intensify as she walked along the drive. Marcus's car was gone, and as she went inside the house seemed to echo with emptiness. Going up to her room, she quickly changed into her swimsuit. Collecting a large towel from the airing cupboard, she went back to the garden. Laying the towel on the grass next to the flagstoned pool surround, she unclipped Peter from his harness and carried him back to the towel. His warm, squirming body gave her a feeling of security—which was utterly ridiculous.

He seemed to remember the water, and began chortling and laughing, struggling to be free. It struck chill at first and she gasped, wondering if it would be too cold for the baby. She didn't want him to get a chill, he'd been very hot the night before. Dithering uncertainly, Peter took the decision from her by almost leaping from her arms and into the water, and with the natural instinct of children that always amazed her he began doggy paddling aross the pool, a beaming smile of satisfaction on his face. Laughing, Toby swam lazily alongside him, ready to offer assistance if it was needed or if he became tired, rather amused by her newly acquired maternal instincts. She was so absorbed with watching Peter, she didn't see Marcus practically sprint across the grass toward them, and the first intimation she had of his presence was his angry voice thundering at her.

'What the hell is going on?' He sounded so totally horrified that for a moment Toby didn't immediately understand to what he was referring. 'Get my nephew out of there!' he grated furiously.

'He's perfectly all right,' she began reassuringly as she noticed his white face. 'Truly . . .'

'Get him out!' he yelled, which so frightened the baby that he promptly disappeared beneath the water with a spluttering cry.

Capturing the squirming little body quickly, she lifted him into her arms, automatically patting his back as she stared up at Marcus in astonishment. 'Don't shout,' she said, pitching her voice low. 'You'll frighten him, and then he'll always associate it with water.'

'Just get him out of there,' he said grimly.

Sighing, she walked across to the steps at the side of the pool, making soothing little sounds to the baby, who fortunately quickly regained his usual sunny nature. As she halted in front of Marcus, she said with quiet sincerity, 'That was very stupid, Marcus. Peter was im no danger whatsoever. On the contrary, he was a great deal safer than out in his pram. I'm . . .'

'Don't tell me I'm stupid,' he grated furiously. 'And don't you ever . . .'

'Marcus,' she put in swiftly, 'will you please listen to me? I'm a fully qualified swimming teacher.'

'You're a what?' he exploded in disbelief.

'A fully qualified swimming teacher. I've taught any number of babies to swim—and never drowned one,' she added, trying to lighten the fraught atmosphere.

'Even newborn babies take to the water like little fish. They have no fear, you see. A baby doesn't question whether he'll drown or not, it's only people . . .' Like you, she was going to say, then changed her mind. There was no need to put his back up any further. 'Adults,' she substituted, 'who transmit fear. See? He's perfectly happy again,' she murmured, turning her eyes to Peter, who was investigating the top pocket of the short-sleeved shirt Marcus was wearing. With a sound of fury, Marcus turned on his heel and stalked back toward the house, and Toby felt a bitter disappointment. Had she so totally misjudged him? she wondered unhappily. Had she been so very blind? She'd always thought him a fair man. Disagreeable sometimes, but fair, and she couldn't believe how much it hurt that she'd been wrong. As Peter gave an enormous yawn, she smiled weakly at him. 'Not very good judge of character, am I?' she asked him, as she walked back toward the house. Perhaps she'd been wrong about Lydia, too. Only that wasn't a thought that brought any comfort.

Rubbing the baby dry and putting on a clean nappy, she lay him down in his cot for his nap. After showering and dressing in a cotton skirt and T-shirt, she idly picked up the guitar. Hadn't done much about becoming Segovia, had she? She'd barely touched it since she'd been here. Not that she felt much like emulating him now. She felt sort of empty and sad. Bit by bit, Marcus seemed to be draining her of her confidence. Yet why should he believe or trust her? She hadn't exactly been Miss Perfection to date, had she?

Walking back into the nursery, she smiled faintly at

Peter, who was sitting up playing with his toes. 'You're supposed to be asleep,' she told him, wryly, and, as he only beamed, Toby settled herself on the floor, her back against the wall. Running her thumb over the strings, she grinned as Peter chortled. 'Like that, do you?' Drawing up one knee to balance the guitar, she began to strum. Only knowing three chords, she was a bit limited for tunes. It was either, 'Oh, dem Golden Slippers' which always reduced Sally to hysterics, 'Freight Train' or 'Froggy Went A-Courting'. Deciding that 'Freight Train' was a bit too advanced for an eight-month-old baby, she began playing 'Froggy'. Her voice was soft but, unfortunately, as out of tune as her playing. As her mother was so fond of pointing out, she couldn't carry a tune in a bucket.

'Is that the only way you can keep an audience, Toby?' Marcus asked softly from the doorway. 'Put them behind bars?'

Starled, Toby quickly turned her head. 'Not very discerning, is he?' she managed weakly.

'Probably tone deaf like his mother,' he observed easily, walking further into the room, yet there was a hint on tension in him—he wasn't nearly as relaxed as he was pretending. As he held his hand out, Toby was too surprised to do anything but pass the guitar across.

'Can you play?'

'There is absolutely no need to sound so incredulous, Toby,' he said drily, setting himself on the floor beside her. 'There are probably any number of things I can do that you don't know about—or suspect,' he added, turning to give her a lazy smile that turned to a wide grin as she only continued to stare at him in absolute amazement.

'You smiled,' she said faintly. 'You actually *smiled*. Properly.' And the difference it made was extraordinary. Devastating, and all she could do was stare at him like an idiot as her heart made a slow, painful somersault.

'I do sometimes,' he murmured, competently re-tuning the guitar

'I've never seen you.'

'No, I only ever do it in private—don't want to spoil my image, do I?' he teased, slanting her a bright glance, his extraordinary eyes actually gleaming with laughter.

'You toad,' she said softly, her own mouth curving into an enchanting smile. 'You little toad. But why?' Had it all really only been an act? His arrogance? His withdrawn behaviour? The horrendous childhood? Had it all been a sham?

'Why?' he exclaimed, breaking off his absent strumming. 'You can actually ask me why? What might I ask have I had to smile about since you so thoroughly disrupted my life?'

Her smile slowly dying, she asked huskily, 'Have I really been that horrendous?'

'Yes, Toby. Very horrendous. I can honestly say that in all my thirty-six years I have never met anyone even remotely like you.'

'I see,' she murmured slowly, and found she had the most ridiculous desire to burst into tears. Ridiculous, because she'd known what he thought about her, hadn't she? Blinking rapidly, she summoned up a lame smile that made her look haunted, then was quite unable to interpret the penetrating glance he gave her.

'He's asleep,' he murmured, laying the guitar aside.

'What? Oh, yes,' Toby mumbled, glancing toward the cot. 'He usually goes off very quickly. Did you want some work done?' she asked and, finding his proximity too unsettling, she scrambled awkwardly to her feet. That was presumably why he had come; she couldn't conceive of any other reason why he should seek her out. As he got to his feet, she walked swiftly over to the window.

'Will you stop dodging away from me?' he said, sounding thoroughly exasperated. 'What in God's name do you think I'm going to do to you?'

'I don't think you're going to do anything,' she said shortly pretending a total absorption in the garden, then stiffening as she felt Marcus move up to stand behind her.

'Actually, I came to aplogise,' he said, causing Toby to swing round in astonishment.

Gazing up at him, her drying hair curling into little wispy ringlets to frame her face, she widened her eyes incredulously. 'Apologise?'

'Mm,' he murmured ruefully, and Toby had the fanciful notion that those bright blue eyes had darkened fractionally. He also seemed rather trans- fixed by the sight of her untidy hair, and she put her hand up in a self-conscious gesture to tidy it.

'Leave it,' he ordered quietly, capturing her hand and moving it aside, yet retaining his hold on it. 'Are you really a swimming instructor?'

'Yes,' she murmured, her throat dry, and she was unbearably aware of his warm hand clasping hers and wasn't sure whether to try and remove her hand or leave it where it was.

'A real, genuine, *bona fide* instructor?'

'Yes,' she whispered, searching his eyes for a double meaning behind the remark, only as usual it was incredibly difficult to read anything from that still face.

'Then I apologise for my behaviour down by the pool. Blame it on my over-zealous guardianship of my nephew. Hm?' he added, with a quirk of one eyebrow.

Giving him a hesitant smile, she wished her heart wouldn't race so, And she had the awful fear that he might touch her, because she didn't know what she would do if he did. She also wished belatedly that she had chosen any part of the room to stand in but the window embrasure where his bulk so effectively trapped her.

'Nervous, Toby?' he queried softly.

'Is it any wonder?' she croaked. 'After last night, I'm never quite sure what you're going to do.' And when he gave a slow, lazy smile that seemed to turn her insides to jelly, and put up his other hand to move the clinging curls away from her face, she visibly flinched.

'That was a very bad mistake on my part. And I don't like making mistakes, Toby Anderson,' he said with a wry twist to his mouth. "I didn't sleep too well, either. Did you?' he asked softly.

'No,' she whispered, unable to tear her eyes away from his.

'I lay awake,' he continued reflectively, causing all sorts of weird sensations to riot inside her, 'and I thought of you. Wondered about you.' As his eyes slid with lazy appraisal to her mouth, Toby took a deep, shuddering breath, almost able to taste that firm mouth pressed to hers. Almost able to feel those strong arms holding her, and without being aware that she did so, she swayed toward him. As his palms slid to press encouragingly against her shoulderblades, she closed her eys, and a moment of exquisite torture passed before she felt his lips capture her own. Not harshly as before, but softly, a butterfly caress that was swiftly gone, only to return, tantalising her with a promise that was not yet fulfilled.

Unable to help herself, she slid her arms round his waist to touch the warm, shirt-clad back Her fingers slid over firm muscles and taut spine, and as his own palms slid to her waist, pressing her closer, Toby parted her mouth in silent invitation. Time seemed to stop, cocooning them, the air still as she explored his mouth, tasted its warmth. As she felt his slow arousal, she raised herself on tip toe to fit her body more accommodatingly to his. Oddly she felt no sense of urgency, only this dreamlike desire to explore and be explored, to exchange soft, pleasurable kisses, to feel his breath on her face, to touch her lips to hard cheekbones, a strong throat. It wasn't until his palms moved to her ribs and his thumbs probed the soft fullness of her breasts that she became consciously aware of what they were doing, and she opened dazed eyes.

'No,' she whispered raggedly, just staring at him, her eyes dark. He wanted her, as she wanted him, she admitted honestly. But it was only want for him. Her feelings, she knew, went much deeper. Should she take what was offered and to hell with tomorrow? Only, what sort of opinion would he have of her then? she thought dazedly. Thoughts and feelings raced crazily through her head as she decided she wanted his good opinion. *Needed* it, she found. Wanted him to like her for herself. And yet not five minutes ago he'd told her she was horrendous. Besides, if she let him take what he seemed to think was on offer, she'd hate herself.

He was leaving the decision to her. He wasn't going to force it, he would just wait, as he was waiting now, his eyes fixed on her face. Quiet, waiting, watchful—and, oddly, that made it easier. If he had been ardent, not giving her a choice, there would have been no decision to make and she supposed she ought to feel grateful. Only, she didn't. She felt achingly empty. It could only have been seconds that they stared at each other, and yet it seemed like for ever. Examining that still face, she wanted to fit her palms against that strong jaw, wanted to press her mouth back to his. Flushing at where her thoughts were taking her, she moved uncomfortably and he gave a rather mocking smile as he read her decision. And that was the only way it could be, she thought bleakly as he released her. Whether the man were rich or poor, the end result would be the same for her. Heartache. For the same reason that she backed away from a relationship with Brian, so too did she from Marcus. Despite his mocking smile, she could see that her behaviour had puzzled him. Yet she couldn't explain, only put a determined clamp on her emotions, bury them. Or try to.

'What is it that you want, Toby?' he asked quietly.

'Want?' she asked helplessly. Then with a deep sigh, said stupidly, 'My lunch, probably.' And her voice came out cracked and wobbly. Pushing quickly past him before she could betray herself further, she went down to the kitchen.

Feeling muddled and unhappy, she forced herself to

prepare lunch and found to her chagrin that her body obeyed its own laws. As Marcus came in, he reached past her to filch a radish from the salad bowl and her body reacted as though bereft from a promise unfulfilled. For two pins she could have hurled the salad bowl across the kitchen. How could she have been so stupid as to think all choices were easy? You made a decision and acted on it, and never before had she been left so confused. And the fact that he seemed quite unbothered by her rebuttal was like bitter gall in her throat.

Moving away from him, she tried to make her actions casual, and knew she'd failed when she caught his bright, penetrating glance. 'I know. Don't say it,' she grated huskily, and he would never know, she thought, how hard it was to appear amused. 'I'm an emotional coward.'

'Or a tease,' he taunted softly.

Staring at him in surprise, because she hadn't considered he might put that interpretation on it, she was about to deny it when she decided it might be best for him to believe that. There could be no future in a relationship with him; she wanted one, but was suddenly determined not to give in to her baser instincts. There was a choice, there had to be. So, why not led him think her a tease? It would stop him probing for deeper motives Toby didn't fully understand herself. Without answering, she finished setting out the lunch.

When they'd eaten, she cleared away and washed up before giving Peter his lunch and putting him back in his pram. When she returned to the garden, it was to find Marcus stretched out on a lounger. His eyes were closed and Toby took the opportunity to study him unobserved, or so she thought. The last few days had wrought a change in him. As they had in her, she thought unhappily. Yet he seemed more relaxed, younger. The frown mark was not so pronounced as previously. She felt as though she'd aged a hundred years.

'Changed your mind?' he suddenly asked, proving he had been well aware of her scrutiny.

'No,' she said hastily. Moving across to the other lounger, she lay back, tilting her face to the sun. When he said no more, Toby gradually relaxed and was almost asleep when he spoke again.

'Time enough for our lunch to have gone down. Come on, lazybones, you can demonstrate this exceptional skill you assure me of.'

Opening her eyes a fraction, she peeped at him warily through her lashes. He was sitting on the edge of his lounger, staring at her. 'Which skill is that?' she murmured with unconscious provocation.

'Swimming,' he said succinctly.

Opening her eyes fully, she stared back at him in bewilderment. 'Swimming?'

'Yes, Miss Anderson. Swimming. You tell me you're a qualified instructor. So prove it. I took you on trust once before, and look where it got me.'

'Ah,' she murmured, sitting up.

'Yes, Miss Anderson, *ah*. Lack of shorthand skill doesn't put life at risk. Lack of swimming very well could.'

Acknowledging the very real truth of that, she nodded seriously as she got to her feet. 'I quite agree. I'll go and get changed.' Her swimsuit was still wet and it was ridiculous how uncomfortable it felt when she'd finally managed to struggle into it. It felt horrible, and she didn't remember that it had ever clung quite so lovingly to her figure before. Surveying herself in the full-length mirror, she groaned in despair. She looked as though she'd been poured into it, and instead of flattening her rather full bust it only seemed to enhance it. It also seemed to make her waist look impossibly tiny, which emphasised the flare of her hips. Well, there was very little she could do about it—so long as he didn't take it as an open invitation to continue where he'd left off. Rather embarrassed by her inspection of herself, she turned away to remove the pins from her hair. Marcus would not be best pleased if one of the clips came out in the water and blocked the filter.

He'd also changed, she discovered, and although she'd seen him almost naked before, she hadn't been in any fit state to take it in. But now the sight of him in brief black swimming-trunks made her halt in shock. She'd always known he would have a magnificent body, his classic suits had never disguised that fact, but now he was almost naked Toby could see just how superb that lithe, tanned body really was. He was standing with his back to her, and she stared with un-ashamed pleasure at the broad, muscled back that tapered down to a narrow waist, lean hips and strong legs, and a flare of excitement curled inside her. As if aware of her presence, he turned, and Toby blushed at the comprehensive glance he gave her.

'No bikini?' he asked, surprised, as she walked rather self-consciously toward him.

'No,' she mumbled, then had to clear her throat.

'Bikinis are apt to come off when diving.' She gave a small, unconsciously cheeky grin as she remembered it happening to her. It had been very embarrassing. Then went pink as he gave her a look that needed no interpretation. However, for whatever reasons of his own, he apparently decided not to embarrass her further.

'Presumably there is also a good reason for leaving your hair loose?' he asked, transferring his gaze to the cloud of toffee-coloured hair.

'There is when it's your pool,' she said wryly. 'I'm in enough trouble as it is without blocking the filter with one of my hair-clips.'

Giving a little smile of agreement, he said, 'So, Miss Anderson. Demonstrate.'

In a swift movement that took him by surprise, Toby executed a perfect racing dive and, as she surfaced nearly half-way up the pool, continued with a flawless crawl that took her swiftly to the end, where she made a professional-looking turn and swam back toward him.

Resting her elbows on the side, she grinned up at him. 'Skilful enough?'

'Very good,' he applauded drily. 'How are you at life-saving?' And, before she could answer, he'd run along the edge of the pool and executed a very credible dive of his own. As he surfaced at the far end and gave a ridiculous demonstration of a man drowning, Toby gave a shout of laughter before swimming toward him, her worries and awareness for the moment buried in the pleasure of being in the pool.

'If you struggle too hard, be warned, I shall render you unconscious,' she muttered sternly, and his only answer was to go limp and disappear beneath the surface. Pulling a face, Toby duck-dived after him. In her element, lithe as an otter, and ignoring the gleam in his eye, she swam round, behind him. With one hand beneath his chin, she took him easily to the surface, then towed him to the side. 'Thank you,' she said softly, shaking wet hair from her eyes.

'For what? Not allowing you to render me unconscious?' he asked drily.

'Something like that,' she murmured, endeavouring to hoist herself out. The movement of the water kept moving her against him so that her legs entangled with his, and was forced to use her arm to keep them apart. A watery embrace with him was the last thing she needed; as it was, she was unbearably conscious of firm, muscled flesh against her own.

'Not so fast,' he murmured, his voice laced with laughter. 'Aren't you suppose to pull me out?'

Turning her head, she stared at him nervously as she remembered just exactly how she had been trained to get an unconscious body from the water. It involved standing on the side and drawing him up one extending leg before turning him over into the recovery position while she checked for heartbeat and lung movement. 'I can do it,' she whispered drily, 'but . . .'

'But you don't want to do it with me,' he finished for her. Giving her a smile that oddly held no mockery, he suddenly boosted her up and out of the water by the simple expedient of placing one large hand beneath her bottom. Joining her on the side, so that they both sat with their feet in the water, he murmured blandly, 'Kiss of life?'

'No! Not that I can't,' she qualified as he burst out

laughing at her vehement tone. 'But because it could be dangerous on someone healthy. The same goes for heart massage.' This was true, but even if it hadn't been she would have pretended it was. Just the thought of deliberately putting her mouth to his, for whatever reason, made her go weak. Rolling away from him, she lay back and tilted her face to the sun, then ran through the whole procedure verbally, just to prove she knew it. And wished she didn't sound so damned breathless. Although, with luck, he might put it down to the exertion of life-saving, and knew even as she thought it that he wouldn't put it down to any such thing.

When he was silent, she turned her head toward him curiously, then gave a little smile of relief as he murmured, 'All right, I will accept that you are qualified to teach my nephew.'

'Thank you,' she said sincerely. 'I promise to take very great care of him.'

'Yes. I don't know why I believe you. But I do.' Then, lying back beside her he asked curiously, 'Why did you lie about your shorthand?' And his words gave Toby a nasty jolt.

Levering herself up with her arms straight out behind her, she stared down into his face, her own expression very serious. 'Because I needed the job,' she said simply. There would never be a better opportunity to tell him about the other lies—and she wanted to tell him. Wanted there to be honesty between them. Taking a deep breath, she began slowly, 'Marcus?'

'Mm?' he murmured, one finger reaching out to trail with seductive slowness along her arm, causing

Toby to give a delicious shiver.

'I . . .' Only, before she could explain, some sixth sense warned her they were no longer alone. Marcus, too, no longer had his whole attention on her, but was looking beyond her, his eyes narrowed.

'Lydia,' he murmured. Then, returning his eyes to her, he said softly, 'Maybe you were right.' And before she could gather her scattered wits he had pulled her across his lap.

'About what?' she asked, startled.

'About my being in love with you, of course,' he breathed before his mouth covered hers and strong arms gathered her against his warm chest. Her immediate reaction was to stiffen in shock, but as his mouth began a gentle exploration of her own she slowly relaxed, melted against him, her arms creeping up and around his neck. It was unbelievably stupid of her, she knew that. With the rational part of her mind that was still functioning she knew she should push him away, but the feel of his mouth on hers, teasing, demanding, made her feel quite incredibly wanton, and she turned fully into his arms.

The reason for the kiss was temporarily forgotten as she gave herself up to the exquisite pleasure of it. As he lay her back on the warm stones, Toby held him to her, moving her body to accommodate his more masculine curves, and didn't care that Lydia was watching. She didn't want to stop him, wanted so much more, and for one crazy moment her hand began to move to touch him, only some remnant of sanity stopped her and she clenched her hand hard against his back. His mouth lifted reluctantly and he raised his head to gaze down into her sleepy amber eyes.

'You are quite incredibly soft and cuddly,' he said thickly, his beautiful eyes bright and intent on hers. 'And you're frustrating the hell out of me. I want to make love to you, possess you uttely—and with infinite slowness.'

'You do?' she croaked, her voice as thick as his own had been.

'Yes. But you aren't going to let me—are you?'

'No,' she whispered reluctantly, her voice barely audible. 'I don't think that would be very wise at all.' And she wondered at his wry smile until he explained.

'Now is not the time I could have wished for wisdom,' he murmured huskily. Getting lithely to his feet, he dived into the pool, leaving Toby feeling unbelievably bereft.

CHAPTER SIX

WAS it only because Lydia had been watching that he'd kissed her? Might it not have been just a little on his own account? He'd said it would be no hardship, hadn't he? Watching that sleek, dark head, the powerful arms cleaving the water, she sighed. Would it have been so wrong to take what was offered? So wrong to let him make love to her? Allow those strong limbs to enfold her? That hard body thrust close to hers? Lying back, folding her arms behind her head, she closed her eyes, his image retained on her retina. With the warm sun on her face, the summer sounds to soothe her, she listened idly to the slap of water against the side of the pool. Nothing was different, the same rules applied. The Marcus du Manns of this world were not for her. Her body was relaxed, yet her mind in turmoil. The feel of him, the taste of him, remained with her. She couldn't be in love with him, that was ridiculous. Wanting wasn't loving. There were so many things about him that were totally unlovable. His arrogance, his autocratic behaviour, his insistence that he was always in the right. Only that wasn't quite true; he'd apologised for misjudging her, hadn't he? Unsettled, Toby got swiftly to her feet and walked across to the loungers. Lying down, she tried to empty her mind and must have succeeded to a certain extent, because she drifted into a light sleep and only woke when she heard the sound of glasses clinking.

Opening her eyes, she squinted up at Marcus. He had the baby in one arm and a tray of glasses in his free hand.

'I brought us some lemon,' he said easily. And, putting the tray on the table, he passed Peter across to her. He still held Peter as though afraid he might bite him and she gave a small smile. Unfortunately, the sight of those two dark heads so close together set up yet another reaction. Peter could have been his son. If he'd married Lydia, they would no doubt have had sons, sons that looked like Peter, and a fierce stab of jealousy shot through her for the woman who might one day bear those sons. Hastily lowering her eyes, afraid he might guess something of her thoughts, she made a great pretence of tidying Peter, straightening his rompers. It took her a while to shake off her melancholy, and she caught Marcus looking at her once or twice, as though trying to understand her mood.

They spent the rest of the day round the pool, and Marcus even took Peter in swimming. She managed, she thought, to behave normally, not letting him guess at the turmoil he had created inside her. This was a different Marcus—relaxed, laughing, an easy companion, one only too easy to imagine herself in love with. Toby admitted quite freely that she showed off. Diving and swimming, wanting, needing him to know that she excelled at something. She knew he was well aware of what she was up to, but she didn't care. Only, she made very sure that they didn't accidentally touch. That their bodies didn't come into contact. He knew that too, she could see the mocking knowledge in his eyes. Yet gradually, against her will, she relaxed, and when Peter had fallen asleep they lay side by side on the towel, faces tilted to the sun, fingers touching. They talked desultorily at first, exchanging little anecdotes, and she admitted with a rueful little smile that with her half-knowledge of him she had coloured in his life to suit her own ideas. An image of Marcus as a student, learning to play the guitar, for the simple reason that it represented a challenge, then being dragged against his will to attend midnight feasts to provide the music, made her chuckle. He could be very amusing. He was a gifted raconteur and a first-class mimic, and soon had her laughing helplessly. They wrangled amiably over politics, music, travel, and if she was surprised by him he equally was surprised by her. She had a very good grasp of many subjects, and a wry perception that amused and intrigued him.

'Well, no one could accuse you of being a dumb blonde, could they?'

'Did I ever pretend I was?'

'Yes, Toby, he said firmly. 'You did.' And, getting lazily to his feet, he extended one hand to pull her up. 'Come on, you look as though you might burn, your face is red.'

Probably guilt, she thought, allowing him to pull her to her feet. She still hadn't told him about the fictitious qualifications. She persuaded herself it was because she didn't want to spoil their present relaxed mood. Only it wasn't altogether that. She had a cowardly impulse not to tell him at all; she didn't think she could bear to see the condemnation in his eyes.

*   *   *

She made scrambled eggs on toast for their tea, and it wasn't until she put Peter down for the night that her nervousness returned. She'd spent other evenings alone with him, only that was before he had kissed her, teased her. Now she was wary of being alone with him. He was beginning to make her feel very young and inexperienced. At least Peter had acted as a barrier. She delayed going down as long as she could, but there was only so much time she could take to shower and wash her hair. She dressed in a cream top with narrow shoulder-straps that enhanced the tan she was beginning to acquire, and a full cream cheesecloth skirt. A warm, enchanting flush lay along her cheekbones, and Toby wasn't sure if the sun had put it there, or her confusion. And he knew, damn him. Knew what he was doing to her emotions. That gleam in his eye told her that.

He was lounging in the armchair, his feet propped on the fender, long legs clad in well-cut grey trousers. His torso was clad in a pale blue shirt, the cuffs rolled back to reveal the strong forearms. His hair was still damp from his shower and curled attractively behind his ears. His teeth gleamed whitely as he taunted, 'Want me to go out?'

'No,' she said stiffly. 'Why should I want that?'

'Oh, I thought you might be afraid I might leap on you. Or afraid that I wouldn't,' he said softly.

'Don't be ridiculous!' she said shortly, throwing herself into the other chair. 'Do you want to play backgammon?'

'Not particularly,' he murmured lazily. 'Do you?'

Giving a little shrug to denote her indifference, she picked up the paper from beside her and buried herself behind it. She heard the little laugh he gave, but was determined to ignore it. All it needed was a bit of common sense, that was all. She might stare at the newsprint that wavered before her eyes, but every sense was attuned to him and she knew exactly the moment that he put his feet down, got up and began walking toward her. You are not in love with him, she told herself fiercely. You do not want him! As he removed the paper from her lazy grasp and perched on the arm of her chair, Toby stiffened.

'Look at me,' he said softly, one hand curling round the back of her neck.

'No,' she said mutinously, and wanted to hit him when he chuckled.

'When I first saw you,' he began, his voice gentle, reminiscent, 'I knew you were going to be trouble. Trouble with a capital T. Do you know what that sexy voice of yours does to a man?'

That did make Toby look up. Staring at him in utter astonishment, her lovely eyes at their widest, she found she didn't know what to say. Sally had said much the same thing, and she'd pooh-poohed the idea. Common sense dictated she didn't believe Marcus either, but that one involuntary look at him revealed eyes that were too bright, too intent, to be ignored.

'Eyes of a jungle cat,' he continued. 'A wide smile that makes a man feel special.'

'No!' she exclaimed huskily. 'No, Marcus.'

'Yes, Toby. Yes, yes, yes, yes, yes.' And, bending his head, he captured her mouth with his own. His lips were warm and dry, insistent, and Toby was helpless. He didn't hold her, the hand on the back of her neck was light, a touch only, she could have escaped quite easily—only she didn't. It was almost as though she were wax and he the flame. All the tension dissolved, her muscles relaxed, her lids dropped as her senses revelled in the warm male smell of him, the tang of cologne, the taste of toothpaste, the warmth of his skin, the touch of his palm on her neck. Parting her lips to him, she registered each separate touch of lip on lip. The soft, drugging kisses he was planting on her mouth, the strong teeth taking first the lower then the upper lip, tantalising, taunting, until with a small groan she arched toward him, her arms sliding up to encircle his neck and pull him down. As though it were a practised movement, he scooped her up and returned her to his lap as he slid into the chair. One warm hand was busy removing the pins from her hair, and he gave a soft sigh as the silky strands tumbled free to frame her face.

'Beautiful, disruptive Toby who haunts my sleep. Did you know that until you came into my life I didn't know how hard I worked? Didn't know I could spend a whole day and not think of the office once? Do you have any idea, I wonder, how much I want to make love to you? How my hands long to touch that warm body?' Toby sucked in her breath hard.

'Marcus, no! Oh, why are you doing this?' she wailed, confusion and want and sensation all warring inside of her. Her body seemed locked in a time warp from which there was no escape. 'You don't even like me, you said so.'

'Like?' he murmured, his mouth a mere hair's breadth away. 'I don't think liking comes into it. I want you. I want to get you out of my mind, and if the only way to do it is to make love to you, then make love to you I will.'

'Don't I have any say in the matter at all?' she asked helplessly, and her eyes searched the deep blue of his for reassurance or help, she wasn't sure which. She was a pawn. She didn't want this to be happening, she wanting to go back to the carefree days of last week. Only it was too late. Far, far too late, and she watched, almost fascinated, as his mouth moved back toward hers and his lashes lowered to lay like silky black fans, hiding his thoughts from her. Toby finally surrendered. Gave up all thoughts of resistence and shame that he didn't want her for love, only to exorcise her from his mind. Tugging his shirt free, she slid her palms inside to touch the warm flesh, and a little sigh that was almost contentment escaped her.

Time blurred and became one frozen moment.

His mouth seemed to find every nerve-ending on her body, and it wasn't enough to lie acquiescent, she needed to participate, be a full partner. As his mouth roved lower, across her flat stomach, Toby began her exploration. She ran her thumbs down the strong spine, finding each pleasure zone with unerring accuracy, the lessons she'd taken in physiotherapy as part of her swimming course standing her in good stead. She no longer felt a part of herself, but a separate being, floating somewhere above, watching, feeling. Toby let out a little cry, clutching him tighter, arching against the exquisite pleasure he was giving her, the force inside her overriding sense, caution, and then they were joined as one, both needing the fulfilment that each had promised.

They lay for a long time, not speaking, just holding each other. His head was in the angle of her shoulder and neck, and her mouth touched his damp hair. As her heart gradually regained its normal rhythm, her breath no longer fighting to get into her lungs, she smoothed damp palms down his back in a soothing rhythm, not wanting it to end, not wanting to admit it was over. Toby needed to hold on to the most beautiful moment of her life for a little longer, to halt time, not have reason intrude and burst the illusion. That was what it was all about, what had been written about since time began. Not just a coupling, not just an animal need, but a shared warmth, a shared joy— love. It should have been for love, it was too beautiful to be called anything else. But Marcus did not love her, not the essential part of her that was unique to herself. And neither was she totally sure that she loved him, she thought sadly. Her heart was full with the need to say it, to exclaim at the beauty of it, the perfection, yet she could not, and her eyes blurred with tears. She had no way of knowing what he thought or felt, but guessed it was a confusion similar to her own. No one could fake the response he'd given. No man could fake the words he'd cried out. Perhaps he too was afraid to speak, to bring it all back to normality. At he stirred and his mouth moved against her neck, a soft butterfly kiss, she slid her hands back to his shoulders and her fingers crept to entangle with his hair.

'Toby?' he murmured softly.

'Mm?'

And then he didn't seem to know what to say because he gave a funny little laugh before levering himself up to look into her face, and his mouth curved into a smile.

'You look delightfully abandoned,' he whispered moving his hand to her face to push away the tumbled hair. A hand that shook, Toby noticed. His voice wasn't any too steady either, and she smiled. He looked and sounded as unlike the Marcus she knew as it was possible to be. His hair was wildly tangled across his forehead and the blue, blue eyes were sleepy, drugged, the mouth soft and sensous, and she felt a renewed curl of desire. He was so impossibly beautiful. The words 'I love you' hovered on her tongue, only to be hastily swallowed. She didn't have the right to love this man, didn't have the right qualifications; and she smiled again sadly before smoothing his hair back with a gentle hand that also shook slightly.

'There's a need, Toby, isn't there? To say words neither of us can say?' And as, she gave a little nod of surprised agreement, he too smiled, a rather lopsided smile that was totally endearing, and her throat locked tight which prevented her speaking at all. A hard lump had formed that wouldn't go away, despite repeated swallowing.

'Beautiful, generous Toby. Toby with the laughing eyes. Toby with the engaging smile that make people want to smile back. What am I to do with you, Toby? I have this awful feeling I'm going to need you very badly.'

'Awful?' she whispered huskily.

'Mm. I have no room in my life for you. I would have said, until now, that I had no feeling. Yet that is quite patently untrue.' Giving a long sigh, he rolled easily to his feet. 'Go to bed, Toby Anderson,' he said softly, looking down at her. 'Take your magic away.'

Staring up at him, at the strong, tanned body, she

closed her eyes for a moment to hide the wash of tears. Then, getting slowly to her feet, she collected up her discarded clothes and went up to her room. She went through all the motions. Washing, cleaning her teeth, putting on her nightie, only to lay awake in the cold bed. Her body still ached from lovemaking; it craved a warm back to snuggle up to. Her arms ached to hold him and she allowed slow, heavy tears to roll unheeded down her face to soak the pillow. How did you take away the magic? she asked herself. Hypnotism?

Was that it? All there was to be? Had he now exorcised her from his mind? And tomorrow, would he revert to Marcus du Mann, boss?

She could hear the clock on the landing tick-tocking away the hours. Could hear the owl, almost hear the rustle of field mice as they went back their nightly business. Did field mice fall in love? she wondered stupidly. Did their furry little bodies ache? Rolling on to her side, she buried her face in the damp pillow, then stiffened as she heard the door click open. Was that what she had been subconsciously awaiting? Rolling on to her back, she stared toward the doorway. Her heart raced and she clenched her hands beneath the covers.

'I can't sleep,' he said softly, his bulk outlined by the faint light from the landing.

'No,' she whispered back. 'Neither can I.' As he walked across the room to stand beside the bed, she caught the gleam of his teeth as he smiled wryly.

'My bed's bigger.'

'Oh, good,' she said lamely, her voice still thick with tears. As he threw the covers back, she got to her feet and stood before him. As he held out a hand, she put her own into it and walked with him out of the room and across the landing. She should have said no, refused. Had she no pride? Seemingly not. There had been no thought of refusing. No desire to resist. She wanted him with a raw hunger that transcended sense.

He hadn't bothered to put the light on, and the room seemed ghostly in the moonlight shining through the window. It highlighted the wide bed with the cover turned untidily down. It silvered the framed print above the headboard, yet left the rest of the room in darkness. As though it were a practised move, she turned into his arms and snuggled almost fiercely against his naked chest. He lifted her easily and lay her on the bed, and their lovemaking was as urgent and demanding as it had been before, with a fierceness and hunger that matched her own. He barely spoke, and neither did she, yet he curved her warm damp body to his and held her tight as they drifted into sleep.

Hours, or maybe only moments, later Toby drifted up out of sleep to find him watching her. His eyes glittered brightly in the dark room, and they made love again with a poignant gentleness. No haste this time, only softness and exquisite pleasure. His kiss was tender, almost loving, and the ache in Toby's heart increased. As he turned over to sleep, Toby curved against his strong, warm back, and slow tears trickled down her face for wanting things she knew she could not have.

When next she woke, it was to find Marcus standing beside the bed, a damp towel round his neck. His hair was wet, little rivulets of water dripping down his face —and he was unashamedly naked. She knew that her eyes darkened as her heart began to race and a curl of excitement spread inside almost like a physical pain.

'Hello,' she whispered huskily.

'Hello,' he replied softly, his eyes fixed on hers. They seemed so impossibly blue, so impossibly beautiful, and it seemed so incredible that he had made love to her. Whispered soft words to her. To her, Toby Anderson. He tossed the towel aside, then climbed slowly into the warm bed, and his strong arms gathered her against him and his mouth decended to hers. It was a kiss of unbelievable sweetness, not soft, not hesitant. Skilful, warm and hard, and Toby's body curved helplessly to his. Her legs entangled with hard, sinewed calves, and as he fitted himself to her the kiss deepened, joining her soul to his for all times. Her body seemed made for his, despite the difference in their heights. There were no bones digging awkwardly into each other, no uncomfortable wriggling to get it just right, it was as though her body waited for just this man, just this hard body, and opened warmly to receive it. His mouth stayed with hers, not passive, not still, moving, demanding, giving, drawing the very core of her to the surface to be examined, welcomed, joined with his. Yet, for him, it was only exorcism, she thought achingly.

As she lay, her face pressed to his chest, her tongue tasting his flesh, he muttered thickly, 'I was to supposed to be in a meeting half an hour ago.' Levering himself upright, an arm either side of her to take his weight, he stared down into her flushed face, his nose almost touching hers. 'What do I say, Toby Anderson? That I was captured by Lorelei?'

'Captured presupposes that you were an unwilling

partner,' she murmured softly. 'Were you unwilling, Marcus?' She desperately wanted him to deny it. But knew that he wouldn't.

'Yes, my little witch, he said huskily. 'I've always been unwilling. I've fought you in my heart, in my mind—and will probably go on doing so, and when you look at me with those great big eyes I have the awful feeling I'm never going to win.' And his eyes were no longer soft and tender. But rueful. Perhaps he didn't know how much he was hurting her, she thought charitably. Perhaps he didn't know that the small flower that had begun to open in her heart had suddenly atrophied. Turned to stone. To stay for ever as a bud, never given the opportunity to open fully.

'You'd best go,' she murmured, trying to summon up a smile. 'Tell them you were with your therapist.'

He didn't seem to notice the pain or the hurt in her lovely eyes, because he gave a soft laugh before rolling easily to his feet, and Toby sat up to watch him as he dressed. Catching a glimpse of the picture above the bed from the corner of her eye, she turned to stare at it. It wasn't a print, as she had thought the night before, but a painting of a man, just the head and shoulders, but it was so like Marcus that it could only be his father. She wondered why, if he had hated him so much, he had his picture above his bed. Then she remembered that it wasn't his bed, but Wanda's.

'My father,' he said, confirming her own thoughts.

'You're very like him.'

'Only in looks, Toby,' he said flatly, coming to stand beside the bed and stare up at it, and his face had hardened, Toby saw, returned to the cold mask he had worn when she'd first met him. 'He was a fool.

Arrogant, domineering—a liar and a fool. He lied to himself, and he lied to others. And for what?' he asked, giving a harsh laugh.

'Maybe he had good reason to lie,' Toby said hesitantly, then jumped in alarm as he exploded.

'There's never any reason to lie! It's a never-ending spiral, Toby,' he said more gently. 'You tell one then you have to tell another to cover up the first and so on until it's out of control. Never lie to me, Toby,' he added, putting one knee on the edge of the bed and putting out a gentle hand to touch her face.

'I already did,' she began unhappily, a cold, dead feeling in her stomach and heart.

Surprisingly, he laughed. 'By omission, yes, Or exaggeration. You did at least admit it was rusty.'

'What?' she asked, confused, staring up at him, a frown pulling at her brows.

'The shorthand—and the cooking, I suspect,' he grinned, ruffling her hair. 'So long as it's nothing worse than that.' Turning away, he began putting his tie on.

Oh, but it is, she thought helplessly, staring at the broad shirt-clad back. Oh, Marcus, it is. Scrambling off the bed, hunting frantically round for her nightdress—as though it mattered one jot whether she was covered or not!—she hastily wriggled into it. Then, standing hesitantly behind him, she knew it had to be said now. Now, before her courage deserted her entirely. 'Marcus?'

'Not now, Toby,' he said quickly, turning away to pick up his jacket. 'Tell me later.'

'No. I have to tell you now,' she said desperately, catching at his arm.

'Darling, I'm impossibly late. Tell me later—I'll try and get back early. Oh, damn, there's the phone. Probably Frank to find out where the hell I am. Answer it, will you? Tell him I've just left.' And, dropping a swift kiss on her nose, he went, and Toby heard the front door slam behind him. Staring unhappily at the closed door, she finally turned away to answer the phone.

It was Wanda, not Frank, and Toby tried hard to sound enthusiastic as she was told that Anthony was out of danger at last. Not by any means better, but well on the road to recovery. Replacing the phone, she walked across to the nursery to see what mischief Peter had got up to. It was well past the time she usually got him up.

She spent the day mooching around until Mrs H exclaimed at her odd behaviour. But the lie between herself and Marcus had now taken on the proportions of the many-headed Hydra, and she wished with all her heart she had never embarked on anything so stupid as to make up qualifications. She should have told him that morning, insisted he listen, then it would have been over. In more ways than one? The time seemed to drag so slowly, too. She felt as though she had lived her whole life in one day, and as five o'clock came and went so Toby became more and more restless. Two or three times she had picked up the phone to ring him and blurt it all out, only to replace it. That was a coward's way. It had to be said face to face so that she could explain properly. If he would give her the chance. There was the rub; Marcus wasn't the most patient man around, and to him no excuse would mitigate the lies she had told. To a man of his wealth, too, it would be hard for him to imagine the desperation that would prompt the making up of qualifications. She didn't suppose he had ever been in the position of not being able to pay his rent.

He eventually returned home at seven-thirty, after Toby had made a poor pretence at eating the meal Mrs H had cooked. Leaping to her feet as she heard the car draw up, she stood hesitantly in the hall. One look at his face disabused her of any notion that he might forgive her if she told him then. The mood he looked to be in, he'd probably have her hung, drawn and quartered. Obviously his meetings had not gone well. She knew they were in the middle of a delicate takeover, and she supposed there had been a setback. But did he have to look as though he'd totally forgotten who she was? That she was so very unimportant?

'Bad day?' she asked huskily, and and felt only a cowardly relief that she could put off her confession. When he only continued to stare at her, his face hard, she swallowed drily before attempting a smile. 'Mrs H kept your dinner hot. Shall I get it for you?'

She hated herself for her weakness. For her placatory tone. Almost begging for him to smile at her. Like her, she thought in disgust.

'No,' he said coldly. 'I have work to do.' And turning on his heel, he disappeared into the study, banging the door behind him.

Biting her lips worriedly, she stared at the wooden panel that divided them. He'd looked as though he really hated her. Even if his meetings had gone badly, there was surely no reason to look at her like that? Taking a deep breath, she turned the study door-handle and pushed it slowly open. He wasn't working at all, he was standing at the window, his back to the room. Closing the door behind her, she leaned back against it, her hair a bright beacon against the dark wood.

'What's wrong, Marcus?' she asked softly, wishing she had the courage to walk up behind him and put her arms around his waist. 'Is it something I've done?' When he didn't answer, only continued to stare out the window, her lips tightened in exasperation. Pushing away from the door, she walked across the room, the cream lawn skirt she had put on specially for him, because he'd once said he liked it, swirling seductively around her legs. Because she had her eyes on him and not on where she was going, she walked too close to the edge of the desk, and her hip caught the pile of papers he had put there. Tutting with annoyance, she bent to pick them up. The force of their fall had cascaded papers everywhere.

'Leave it!' he said shortly, turning to stare at her.

'Don't be silly, Marcus. It won't take a minute to pick them up.'

'I said, leave it!' he snapped, striding over to haul her to her feet; only, Toby was too quick for him. Moving aside, she picked up the last paper and froze. It was a CV for someone named Sandra Bennet. Who the hell was Sandra Bennet? Turning over the top page, aware without looking up that Marcus was watching her, she read the first few lines—and then she knew. Sandra Bennet was a top secretary from one of London's exclusive secretarial agencies.

Lifting her eyes to him, she whispered slowly, 'She's to be your new secretary?'

'If she proves suitable,' he said flatly.

'Oh, Marcus, why didn't you tell me?' she asked sadly. Especially after last night, she wanted to add. Or was it because of last night? Had he decided that the sooner he got rid of her the better? Unwilling, he'd said. Was that it? Had he spent the day wondering how to escape from her? Swallowing the sob that rose in her throat, she put the CV on the desk. Giving a broken little laugh, she said croakily, 'I was trying so hard, too. Ironic.'

'Ironic?' he bit out furiously. 'My God! Did you think I wouldn't find out? That I wouldn't check?'

'Check?' she said stupidly.

'Yes, Miss Anderson! Check!' And, taking an envelope from his inside pocket, he tossed it on to the desk between them.

Feeling sick, she stared at it as though hypnotised, then slowly reached out to pick it up. Could fate really be so unkind as to let him find out the very day she had tried to tell him? Had *intended* to tell him? Removing the letter from the envelope, she slowly unfolded it, and shivered. In bold black letters across the top of the page was the name of her old school. Chewing the inside of her lip, she read the first few lines before carefully folding it and replacing it in the envelope. 'There were reasons,' she said slowly, fixing her eyes on his in a mute plea for understanding.'

'Oh, yes, Miss Anderson, reasons!' he said bitterly. 'Purely selfish, mercenary reasons!'

Were they? she wondered unhappily. Yes, she supposed they were. Selfish, anyway. She wasn't sure that mercenary came into it, but selfish, yes, she had to admit that. She remembered how she had laughed with Sally. How confident she had been then. But that had been before it mattered so much. 'I'm sorry,' she whispered helplessly.

'Yes, I dare say you are,' he said nastily. 'Now. And for God's sake stop looking at me like that!' he burst out angrily. 'You don't even have the saving grace of having failed the exams! You never even took them!'

'Maybe I took them after I left school,' she murmured, without any clear idea of why she said anything so stupid.

'Did you?' he asked flatly, as though he knew even then that she hadn't.

'No,' she whispered miserably.

'No,' he repeated. 'Oh, get out of here,' he said wearily slumping down into his chair.

Walking slowly across the room to the door, she turned to face him. She felt numb. 'How did you know?' she whispered.

'Know? Know what?' he demanded, his total disillusion stamped clearly on his face.

'My reasons for lying?' she asked, her voice even more husky than usual. Only Sally had known, and she couldn't imagine that he had rung her flatmate.

Leaning back in his chair, he gave her a look of disparagement that hurt her unbearably. 'It wasn't difficult; did you think that no one had overheard your remarks to Frank Dawson? Or that they wouldn't tell me? And do we really need to hold post mortems?' he asked nastily.

'Yes,' she said positively, 'because it doesn't make sense. I didn't tell Frank Dawson my reasons. I didn't tell anyone. Only Sally knew.'

'Sally? Who the hell's Sally?'

'My flatmate,' she murmured. 'I just don't understand how you could know about the rent.'

'Rent? What rent?' he exploded. 'And for God's sake will you stop looking like a damned tragedy queen! What did you expect? That I'd pat you on the head and say never mind? It wasn't only one lie!' he yelled, thumping forward in his chair. 'It was a whole army of them! And to say no one knew was a wonderful self-deception on your part—if that's what it was, which I'm inclined to doubt! The whole office probably knew!'

'But I didn't tell anyone,' she repeated faintly.

'Oh, for goodness' sake! You were overheard, damn it! The very first day you were there you said it was a double bonus. Not only good money, but a . . .'

'Young, attractive boss,' she finished for him as she remembered her foolish words to Frank Dawson, and she didn't need to ask who'd told him. Nina. She was the only one at the office who might delight in spreading rumour and gossip. 'And you thought that was why? I see. I don't suppose it's any use telling you it was a joke?' she asked, lifting troubled eyes to his face.

'No. I can see it won't. Yet that's all it was.'

'And the statement that I adored you, really? That my bad temper was just to throw people off the scent?'

So he had overheard. 'Yes, that too,' she sighed. 'Oh, Marcus, do you really think I have such a high opinion of myself? That I arrogantly assumed myself capable of snaring you in my net? I'm hardly Sophia Loren,' she added, giving a hollow laugh. 'And did you really think I was stupid enough to think you a pushover?'

'How the hell should I know what you think? All I

know is what I was told. But whatever the reasons, or excuses, you lied to me. That's what I can't forgive. My God, it was only this morning I asked you not to lie.'

'That was when I tried to tell you,' she began miserably, 'and by the pool the day before. I know I lied, Marcus, but not for the reasons you seem to think.' When he refused to answer, she walked over to stand beside him. Then, finding it almost impossible to discuss it when she was standing above him, she knelt on the floor beside his chair, her hands on the arm. 'I know you're angry and disgusted and everything,' she began earnestly, 'but you're not thinking straight. How could I have known what you were like when I made up the qualifications? They wouldn't have been because I wanted to trap you. All I knew from the advert was that I would be working for the chairman. I didn't know what you looked like, how old you were, anything. I didn't suddenly think, oh, wow, chairman of a company, he'll be worth pursuing. It was all done on the spur of the moment!' she said urgently. 'I only rang on the off chance when I could find nothing else in the paper, and because I was desperate, and maybe a little crazy. When you told me what qualifications were needed, I said that was OK, I had them.' And she had then typed up the stupid CV, she remembered. 'But that was all, Marcus, truly.' Laying her hand hesitantly on his arm, she flinched when it was roughly shrugged off. He wouldn't even look at her, but stared resolutely ahead, and Toby wasn't even sure if he was listening. He'd made up his mind as to her motives, and that was that.

Staring at the hawklike profile, she gave a long, deep sigh, before getting to her feet. Maybe he'd be in a more reasonable frame of mind in the morning. 'Am I to stay to look after Peter?' she asked quitely.

'Until I can make alternative arrangements, yes,' he said coldly.

'It didn't occur to you that I might just pack up and leave? Cut my losses?' she asked. After all, it would have been quite in keeping with the opinion he seemed to have of her.

'It occurred to me, yes. But despite your penchant for lying, you seem fond of him.'

'Not totally beyond redemption, then,' she murmured with a sad little smile.

'Oh, for God's sake!' he exploded. 'Did you think I'd be amused? That I would enjoy being taken for a fool?'

'No,' she said quietly. 'But whatever you may think, it was only done in desperation because I was behind with the rent, and my words to Mr Dawson were only said in fun. You know what I'm like! I never intended to make a fool of you, Marcus,' she said earnestly. When he didn't answer, only picked up his pen, she stared helplessly at him. And yet, was she the only one with suspect motives? Desperately needing to know, yet terrified if the answer, she asked softly, 'And the lovemaking? Surely that must convince you that . . .'

'That, like all women,' he interrupted scathingly, his eyes like chips of blue ice, 'you're a damned good actress! And don't denigrate it by calling it love! Sex is what it was!' Turning his cold face toward her, he added with flat finality. 'I'm only human. Why shouldn't I take what was so blatantly offered? And why crib about it now? It was, after all, what you'd been leading up to ever since you walked into my office that first morning. You taunted—and you got exactly what you asked for.' Holding her eyes for a moment, he added with a sneer, 'So we both satisfied our curiosity, didn't we?'

As Toby's eyes filled with tears, she whispered brokenly, 'I should hate you for that, shouldn't I?' Closing her eyes tight in pain for a moment, she then walked carefully across the room; she felt as though she might shatter into a million pieces. Closing the door quietly behind her, she leaned back against it for a moment. She was shaking so hard, she didn't think her legs would support her to walk upstairs.

So that was that. Didn't need to be svelte and sophisticated, did you? she asked herself. Virtually dragging herself up to her room, she stared at her reflection in the mirror. Hardly an image of a *feeme fatale*, was it? With her hair escaping the topknot, as usual, her face almost haunted, and her amber eyes much too big for her small face. She looked like some poor old pussy-cat. How on earth could he possibly have thought she had a hope in hell of interesting him? Lorelei. Captured. Witch. Not that she had unconsciously trapped him, but had deliberately set out to do so. And if he hadn't found out about her lies? Would he have continued with the relationship? Until he grew bored? What lies had his father told, she wondered, to make Marcus hate him so? And she watched, almost fascinated, as tears ran silently down her face and dripped from her chin.

The night seemed very long, and Toby didn't think she'd slept at all. Despite her intention to speak to

Marcus in the morning, she found that when it actually came to it she didn't have the courage. If she didn't face him, didn't have to confront that harsh face, she could pretend he'd thought over her words and forgiven her. Except that the angry slam in the front door hardly denoted a man who had forgiven.

'Oh, good grief!' Mrs H murmured when Toby walked into the kitchen. 'Another one. What on earth have the two of you been up to?'

'Only me, Mrs H. Only me. Marcus plays by the rules. All rigidly laid out and adhered to,' she said, a trifle bitterly. 'I've been tried, judged, and sentenced.'

'Well, he didn't look as though he'd been playing, rules or no. He looked as though his favorite dog had just turned round and bit him. He was also in a filthy mood.'

'Yes, he would be,' Toby murmured dispiritedly.

'Going to tell me? Or am I to be left in suspense?'

Giving a wan smile, accepting the cup of tea that was passed to her, Toby took a deep breath. 'I told him a lie.'

'And he found out?'

'Yes.' Lifting heavy lids, she quickly explained, then gave her reasons for doing so. 'I stupidly didn't think he'd check, you see. And if he had,' she admitted honestly, 'it wouldn't have mattered then.'

Only it does now?' Mrs H asked sympathetically, and Toby was horrified to find her eyes fill with tears. Unable to answer, she stared down into her cup, then shut her eyes tight as the tears overspilled and plopped into the tea.

'Ah, lassie, lassie,' Mrs H clucked, breaking her self-imposed rule not to get involved in other people's affairs. 'You've to go?'

'Yes.' Toby sniffed, searching in her dressing-gown pocket for a tissue. 'When he's found someone else to look after Peter.'

'Well, as long as it's not the dratted Lydia,' Mrs H snorted, which at least made Toby smile. 'What will you do?'

'Don't know,' she muttered. 'Shoot myself?' she queried.

'Oh, that'll help,' the housekeeper said drily. 'Go on, go and have a nice bath, get dressed. I'll walk down to the village with the baby and get all the papers. Bound to be something in the situations vacant column. Go on,' she insisted as Toby hesitated, then blushed furiously as Toby leaned across the table to drop a kiss on the lined cheek.

'Thank you, Mrs H,' she whispered huskily, more touched then she would have thought possible by the housekeeper's kindness.

Yet despite Mrs Henson's optimism there was nothing in the papers that was suitable; there weren't even any vacancies for copy typists, which she was qualified for. And most certainly nothing for a swimming instructor. In desperation, she rang each paper in turn to find out how much it would cost to advertise her own services, only to find that she couldn't even afford that. She then rang all the sports complexes and councils within commuting distances of the flat. And finally, employment agencies, leaving the number of the flat and Marcus's house, just in case they found something within the next day or two.

Perhaps she should give up, she thought despondently. Maybe she should go and stay with her mother, only that didn't seem very fair, sponging on her. But then, it wasn't very fair to sponge on Sally, either. If she registerd for unemployment, it would be six weeks before she got the money, and even then it wouldn't be enough for the rent she owed. Maybe she was eligible for social security. And at the rate she was going, she owe a furtune in telephone calls, too.

At Mrs H's insistence, she spent what was left of the afternoon lying in the garden. She managed to eat a light salad for tea, unable to face the thought of dining with Marcus, even supposing he was inclined to dine with her, which wasn't very likely. However, pride did at least dictate that she washed and changed before he was due home. As she left her bedroom, seeing the master bedroom door open, she walked inside. Marcus's father seemed to look down sympathetically at her, and she walked across to stand before the portrait. 'He didn't forgive you, did he?' she asked. 'Didn't come to accept you fallibility. You were ostracised for ever.' How could she love a man who was so rigid? So implacable? Yet she did. She knew that now. You couldn't love to order, as she had once so arrogantly assumed, and now, when it was too late to matter, she discovered just why her mother had continued to love her father after the accident. If Marcus were struck down, which heaven forbid he never was, but if he lost his money, his company, she didn't think she would care a damn, but move heaven and earth to ensure that at least he was comfortable, as happy as she could make him. Dragging in a deep breath to stop the tears that threatened, and holding it until she had herself under control, she went downstairs to sit in the lounge. She didn't think she had felt so damned miserable in her entire life.

She heard him come in; she could hardly avoid it, half the village must have hard the resounding crash the front door made, and her spirits sank even further if that were possible. Obviously a day brooding on her culpability hadn't brought any lightening to his spirit. The crash of the study door followed soon after, and Toby felt a cowardly impulse to run upstairs and hide in her room. Mrs Henson had already left, not that the elderly housekeeper would have been much protection. As she heard his footsteps crossing the hall, she stiffened, then glanced warily at the door as it opened. He looked murderous, she decided. He didn't speak, merely strode across the room and tossed the folded paper on to her lap.

Glancing down in puzzlement, she picked it up gingerly, almost as though it might bite her. 'Read it,' he gritted.

Staring at the columns of print and finding nothing that might clarify things, she turned it over, and there in black and white was the headlines, 'Hi-Tech Takeover'.

'It was made public?' she asked, confused. She hadn't thought negotiations had got that far.

'Dear God, but you're unbelievable,' he said incredulously. 'You have the utter gall to sit there like Alice in Wonderland and ask me that! Do you have any idea of the enormity of what you've done?' he shouted, making Toby jump and cringe back in her chair. 'How many heads will roll? The small investors who've lost money?'

'All because I couldn't pay the rent?' she asked in astonishment.

'Yes!' he hissed. 'All because you couldn't pay the rent! Because you couldn't have what you wanted! Because you were found out! How much did they pay you, Miss Anderson? Enough?'

'Are you insane?' she whispered.

'Insane?' he gritted savagely, dragging her bodily out of the chair. 'Yes, Miss Anderson. I'm insane—with rage! Boy, you really took me for a ride, didn't you? Even after all you'd done, I assumed you had some sort of integrity.'

'I *do* have integrity!' she shouted, wrenching herself free. 'All right, so my shorthand was lousy! My English not brilliant! And I couldn't damn well cook! And I lied about a few lousy qualifications! Does that make me some sort of Judas? You're accusing me of this?' she yelled, striking him on the arm with the rolled-up newspaper that was still clenched in her hand. 'You think I leaked it to the papers?'

'Oh, I don't *think,* Miss Anderson, I *know.*' And, grabbing her arm, he pulled her across the room and into the study. Picking up the pad she had been using and which was still lying on the desk where she let it, he thrust it into her hand. The list of newspapers she had rung to enquire about adverts stared up at her.

Staring from the pad to Marcus and back again, she swallowed the sickness in her throat. 'And that's it? Conclusive proof, Marcus?'

'Pretty conclusive, wouldn't you say?'

'No. I wouldn't call it conclusive at all,' she said brokenly. Tossing the pad back onto the desk, she turned to walk out, her vision blurred by tears. How could he think that of her? How could he?

CHAPTER SEVEN

'OH, NO, Miss Anderson,' he gritted furiously, 'you don't get away that easily!' Striding over to the door, he slammed it shut.

Like a stag at bay, Toby turned and struck his hand away from her. 'You go to hell, Marcus du Mann!' she shouted. 'I no longer owe you anything! I lied to you, yes!' she hissed, his accusations serving to stiffen the backbone that had been in danger of disintegrating. 'I apologised! Not that that makes it right, I know that—but I've paid for that error! Boy, have I paid for it! Only I'm damned if I'm going to stand here and be accused of something I didn't do! Nor would ever do! Being accused of that sort of vindictive behaviour makes me feel sick!'

'Then who did?'

'How the hell should I know? Is it so inconceivable that someone wishes you or the company ill? That someone out in the wide and wonderful world actually doesn't give a damn for Marcus du Mann?' Taking a deep, steadying breath, she fixed wide, tear-washed eyes on his face, then managed more quietly, 'The fact that you could actually consider for one moment that I would deliberately sabotage all the work you and everyone else has put into the merger, for some form of petty revenge, disgusts me! I should pity you, Marcus. Pity you for the lack in your nature that decrees you should look for the worst in everyone. For being unable to trust your own judgement.'

'Oh, there I *will* agree with you,' he said grimly. 'Look how I took you on trust!'

'Yes! And I was loyal to you! In my own way, by my own code of ethics, of which you seem dismally lacking. Because I'd lied, I tried extra hard to please you, to be efficient.' Then she lashed out almost hysterically when he gave a harsh laugh, and her voice broke for a moment as she remembered the struggles she'd had with the typewriter. 'Yes, *tried*!' she yelled, incensed. 'I may not have succeeded, but I tried damned hard! I'm fully aware of what I did, and believe me, no one regrets it more than I, but at least I don't automatically assume that everyone I meet is on the make! At least I have trust!'

'Well, of course you have trust,' he stated bitterly. 'You have no reason not to! It's everyone else who has to watch out!'

Staring at him in disbelief, at the harsh, almost cruel face, she whispered, 'You bastard! Oh, you lousy bastard.' Needing to hit back, hurt him as he'd hurt her, she taunted, 'Is that why your father lied, Marcus? To cover up your own inadequacies? To hide the fact that his son had no soul? No wonder you hated and despised him. He was the one person who could see through your act! And what of your mother? Did she lie, too? And Lydia? Did her defection stem from something other than greed?'

In the sudden awful silence that followed, her words seemed to hang between them, unanswered, unacknowledged, except by the bitter twist to his mouth, the bleak whiteness of his face, and she wished with all her heart that she had not said them. She hated herself for her need to lash out, hated him for making her and was terrified of the violence she seemed to have unleashed.

'Get out of here!' he grated, his voice as low and intense as her own had been.

'Why?' she said bitterly. 'Can't take it, Marcus? All right to dish it out, isn't it? But when it affects your precious life, your character, it's different, isn't it?'

With a violent movement that made her flinch, he slammed his fist into the wall beside her head and, thrusting his face close to hers, he bit out with soft intensity, his blue eyes hard and bright, 'You want to know about my mother? All right, I'll tell you about my mother. She was beautiful, soft, feminine—and an absolute bitch. She married my father for his money and she couldn't even give him fidelity in return. She didn't even bother to be discreet. And my father lied for her, lied to himself and to others.'

'Because he loved her?' she whispered, afraid and bewildered by the tide of bitterness she seemed to have unleashed. 'If it was for love, then he probably didn't have a choice. You don't love to order, Marcus,' she said a trifle bitterly, as she knew to her cost.

'Love?' he asked with a harsh laugh. 'My father never loved anyone in his life! I don't think he was capable of it. He lied for the name. The name was all,' he gritted.

'Then maybe that was why your mother sought love elsewhere . . .'

'How can you be so damned charitable!' he burst out. 'She was little better than a whore!'

'And you can't forgive her any more than you can

forgive me, can you? Because you think I'm the same.'

'Well, aren't you?' he asked, his mouth twisting. 'You lie and you cheat and you smile your smiles . . .' His voice catching, he swung away from her and went to stand at the window. 'Just like Lydia,' he continued more quietly. 'Hedging her bets, keeping her options open. Why in God's name did you have to lie?' he burst out, swinging to face her. 'I didn't want to like you, be beguiled by your charms. I fought so hard against it.'

'My God! Anyone would think I put a blasted spell on you! You think I didn't fight?' she demanded. 'Believe me, Marcus, I fought every bit as hard as you. So much emotion, so much tension—and for what?' she asked bleakly. 'You forced the issue . . .'

'And now I'm reaping the reward,' he said bitterly. 'Well, never again.'

'No, never again,' she echoed silently. She found it inconceivable that her mother had actually married again, for love. Wasn't once enough? 'Why did you force it?' she asked, hating herself for the need to know.

'Because I wanted you,' he said flatly. 'You were driving me insane with your taunts, your teasing—and I wanted you. You gave me a glimpse of the youth I never had. A glimpse of what it might be like to have a laughing wife, a child—and I began to believe that you were different. Only, I should have remembered that to people like you it's only a game.'

'There you go again! *People like me.* What people like me?' she demanded in exasperation. 'I'm me! Not a follower of some fad! I told you why I lied, and it's your damned arrogance that won't accept it, not me playing games! You close up, shut people out, all because you can't accept people as they are! You have to make issue of something that's quite simple!'

'Simple?' he exploded, whirling round to face her. 'You think it's simple that people will lose job'? Investors will lose money?'

'I'm not talking about the blasted merger!' she shouted. 'I'm talking about your lack of ability to trust!'

'Oh, no, Toby. *I'm* not the one with the problem. *You're* the one who probes and prods into motives, backgrounds. Life might be a hell of a lot simpler all round if you minded your own business, looked to your own concerns instead of everyone else's. You're the one who has trouble sorting fact from fiction. What the hell do you think gives you the right to nose around in other people's lives?'

'Taking an interest is not nosing around! And if living in a capsule makes people turn out like you, then it's hardly an example I'd wish to follow!'

'No, more's the pity!' he bit out.

Yet didn't she do just that? she thought bleakly as he turned back to the window. Live in her own private bubble? And she had pried into his life, hadn't she? But she hadn't cheated him, not in the way he meant, and to blame her for something she hadn't done . . . Alter the facts to fit . . . Giving a shuddering little sigh, her feelings so terribly confused, she just stared at him. She loved him—and she thought she hated him as well. She felt guilt and compassion in equal measure. And he—well, he looked as though he had been everlastingly damned.

'I sat in meetings today,' he began, almost as

though words were spilling from him unheeded,
unwanted. 'I listened, talked, presumably made sense,
and all the time I was thinking about you. About your
lies. Hating you. And I kept thinking, how could you
be so blithely confident, so cheerful, when you were
living a lie? How could I have been so stupid as to
want you? Do you know what hurt the most?' he asked
almost conversationally, turning back to face her? 'Do
you? That had been so gullible! When I first met you,
I knew what you were. An empty-headed little fool. A
spoilt little girl who'd always had her own way, had
men at her feet, at her bidding. I knew that!' he
shouted, making her jump. 'How in God's name
could I have been so stupid as to discount it? Then, to
cap it all, before I'd even had time to come to terms
with that, the evening paper carried news of the
merger.'

'And you found the oh-so-incriminating list of
newspapers—and good old Toby was suspect number
one,' she sighed. Staring at him, at the blue eyes, so
cold and condemning, she wondered why she
bothered. Pushing wearily away from the door, she
walked across the room to face him. 'I rang them,' she
said flatly, 'about job advertisements.' When he didn't
answer, only stared at her, almost as though she were
speaking a foreign language, she went on drearily, 'I
understand why lies were anathema to you, because of
Lydia, because of your parents, and I freely admit that
lying isn't quite the best way to make friends and
influence people. I foolishly did not think it would
matter, you see. So in that respect, yes, I was empty-
headed. Or thoughtless. It was not a malicious attempt
to screw up your life. Not an amusing game to cheat

you, inveigle you into my grubby little paws, which is just too ludicrous for words. Apart from which, you stated very clearly that you had no feelings for me. That was a lie, wasn't it? It has to be, otherwise this whole conversation is pointless.'

'You know damn well it was! But there's a hell of a lot of difference between lying for pride's sake and lying just for the hell of it!'

'I lied,' she gritted between clenched teeth, 'because I couldn't pay the rent!' God, how many times did she have to say it? 'Now, to you, not being able to pay the rent is inconceivable, a something not to be considered. To me, it is like a game of tag. Except that everyone else in the game is an Olympic athlete, and you are crippled. You never catch up. No matter how hard you run, dodge, duck and dive, you—don't— ever— catch—up!' she enunciated coldly. 'The reason . . .'

'I don't want your damned reasons!'

'Well, you're going to get them!' she yelled, suddenly losing her temper, and when he looked as though he might interrupt, she said fiercely, 'Shut up!' As he clamped his mouth into a tight line, she began quietly, 'My father was self-employed. When I was fifteen he fell from the roof of a house, damaged his spine. He was left paralysed from the waist down. I loved my father, Marcus. I did,' she said strongly, as though she needed to convince herself. 'But night after night of sitting up with him while my mother worked wore the love a bit thin. When you're nurse, mother, confidante, it's sometimes very hard to remember how close you had been. I had to wash him, change his soiled bed, and each night I was terrified that he would die. Die when there was no one but me to cope. I was fifteen, Marcus.'

'But surely the doctor . . .' he began.

'No! Dad wouldn't let the doctor get a nurse in, a stranger, and I said I could cope. What else could I say?' she demanded wretchedly. 'He was my father, Marcus!' Only, what she hadn't considered was that talking about it would bring it all too vividly to mind. She had never spoken of it until now. Not in detail. To Sally she had only ever given the sketchy outlines. She didn't see Marcus, the study, but her father lying in bed, petulant, demanding. Felt the anguish too, the pain and the fear, and, as though it had all been dammed up too long, it all came spilling out.

'I had to leave school at sixteen without taking my exams. I had to go to work. I worked all day, my mother worked all night, as a cleaner, as a barmaid, then from midnight to eight in the morning in the all-night garage on the till. As she came home at eight-thirty, so I went to work. Even with us both working there was never enough to pay the bills. My father had no insurance to cover the accident, and being self-employed he wasn't entitled to state benefit. Do you have any idea how traumatic it is to be dunned by the gas man, the insurance man, have the electricity cut off? Do you have any idea what it feels like never to have enough money to pay the mortgage, the rates? No, of course you don't. People like you can't conceive of being without cash,' she said bitterly, suddenly focusing on the expensive suit, the gold watch.

'Oh, Toby——' he said helplessly.

'No!' she yelled, startling him. 'I didn't tell you because I wanted your pity! I told you so that you would understand why never again would I let myself be put in that position. Why I needed to lie! You asked me how I could be cheerful, confident. It's because there's no other way to be! Do you think I didn't see enough of my father's self-pity to know what it did to other people? How friends disappear one by one? Well, I don't want anyone's pity!' she said fiercely. 'I'm a fighter, Marcus—and I'll cope by myself, and if it means I have to make up qualifications, then I'll make them up! But that doesn't mean that I would jeopardise other people's jobs! It doesn't mean that I leaked your merger! It doesn't mean that I play games with people's feelings!' Taking a deep, shuddering breath, she went on brokenly, her wide eyes luminous with unshed tears, 'I'd rather be me than you! Too rigid to see anyone else's point of view, or that black and white can sometimes be a dirty grey! It's also why I fought so hard against liking you! I don't want that sort of emotion in my life! I watched my mother turn from a pretty woman into a hag! I watched her despair, her hurt! I watched her love for my father stretched until it almost broke! Well, I don't want that for me! I don't want to feel! And if being shallow, light-hearted, is a way to avoid heartbreak, then I'll be shallow! You keep your rigid principles, Marcus, and I hope you never have cause to regret them!' Dragging a deep breath into her lungs, she whirled away from him and made for the door. With her hand on the latch, she swung back, her face white, strained. 'Did you ever ask your mother why she behaved as she did? Did you? No, of course you didn't. No more than you asked me why I lied. You don't look beyond the facts, do you? That's how it looks, so that's how it is,' she whispered. Unable to face him any longer, unable

to look into that blank, empty face, into those
beautiful, haunted eyes, she fumbled her way out, her
vision blurred by helpless tears. She couldn't take any
more.

Nearly falling in her haste to escape, she ran blindly,
without conscious thought, out through the kitchen
and into the garden, needing to put as much distance
between herself and Marcus as she could. As she
skirted the little copse that bordered the pool, she
caught her foot in a root and stumbled. Her headlong
flight halted, she sank to her knees and huddled
miserably against the tree trunk. The dying sun hung
like a red ball in the sky, its reflection shimmering in
the pool like blood. Fresh tears spilling into her eyes,
she gripped her bottom lip hard between her teeth to
stop its quivering. Holding her breath in her lungs, she
opened her eyes very wide in an effort to halt the tears.
So much pride, she thought brokenly. In both of them.
She to cope, be strong, pay the rent. He had to hide
what he considered weakness, deny his feelings. Yet
where had all her proud honesty gone when she'd lied
to get a job she wasn't qualified for? Her outburst to
him hadn't really been in mitigation, it had been an
excuse. Yet wasn't he as bad? Unable to trust? No, she
admitted honestly, letting her breath out. No. Her
behaviour had been far worse. The end never justified
the means. And what reasons had she ever given him
to trust her? When had she ever shown him that she
could be a responsible person?

She'd made light of his responsibilities to the firm,
she'd blithely set about demolishing Lydia. Arrogantly
championed the window cleaner, the villagers. Had
she ever championed Marcus? No. She'd poked her

nose in where it wasn't wanted, then blamed him for her own shortcomings. Hugging her updrawn knees, she lowered her head on to them, her tears soaking the soft material of her skirt. She felt drained, empty. They'd both said too much, exposed their vulnerability. Yet maybe they'd needed to exorcise their ghosts. They were both in their own way emotional cowards—and she'd proved to be the catalyst, after all. For someone who always backed off from emotion, she'd really gone to town with a vengeance. And look at her now. Sitting in the shrubbery like some defeated garden gnome!'

As the sun finally sank, she shivered. She felt chilled to the bone, yet she didn't want to go back inside. Didn't want to have to face him.

'Toby?'

Closing her eyes in defeat, she huddled closer against the tree. No doubt he now felt guilty too, she thought drearily. Only, she couldn't allow him to think she had thrown herself in the pool in remorse—or an excess of guilt. Getting stiffly to her feet, scrubbing her fists across her stained cheeks like a child, she gave a long sniff before walking back toward the house. He was standing on the lawn, a statue. He looked forbidding and cold, until she reached him and looked into his eyes. They were empty. He looked as defeated as she felt. The soft breeze was ruffling his hair, and she thought, this is how I'll remember him. His beautiful eyes were empty. Is that what I did? Destroyed him too?'

'I'm sorry,' she whispered as she went to walk past him.

'Toby?' he said, once, his hand extended as though

to halt her.

'No more, Marcus. Please, no more,' she murmured, her voice echoing her exhaustion. 'No more.' This way was best. Finish now. It should never have started. She'd known that. She didn't have the strength or the courage of her mother. When the going got tough, she crumbled. An emotional cripple, like her father. Even if she and Marcus talked, it would solve nothing. He did not love her. He'd wanted her, her body, her youth maybe, but not her. Didn't even really want her in his life. She'd put her emotions back into cold store. And there they would stay. Please God.

Walking heavily along the hall, she dragged herself upstairs to her room, where she threw herself across the bed to cry quietly into the pillow.

She left the following morning, after Marcus had left for work. She couldn't even bear to see Peter; she thought she'd fall apart completely if she did. Mrs H took one look at her puffy, tear-stained face, and said nothing. She felt guilty at leaving the housekeeper to cope with the baby, but she couldn't stay. She couldn't trust her voice to say all the things she wanted to say to Mrs H, thank her for her kindness, so she gave her a fierce hug that she hoped said it all, then went quickly out to the taxi. Her last view of the house was of the sun gilding the funny turrets and of the elderly, and suddenly rather frail-looking lady standing on the steps. Giving a sad little wave, she turned her face firmly to the front.

She had no clear idea in her mind of what she would do, but as it turned out, she didn't even have to think about that. When she entered the flat, the telephone was ringing. It was her mother. The sports complex near where she lived needed a temporary swimming instructor, probably for a month. Was Toby interested? Toby was. She left Sally a note to say a job offer had come up in the North. She'd write. Or ring. And then she did neither except to send the money for the rent which she'd reluctantly borrowed from her mother.

She kept herself to herself at the sports complex, earning herself the reputation of being cold, standoffish. There was no trace at all of the gaminé charm that had been such an integral part of her. She took on all the extra duties she could in an effort to exhaust herself, be able to sleep at night, blank it all out. Only, it didn't work. The pain didn't get any better. Worse, if anything. Which was ridiculous. She'd barely known him two weeks, yet common sense and logic refused to banish him from her mind. Her body ached with the punishing routine she persisted in following. She lost weight, dark shadows appeared beneath her lovely eyes. And he was still there: his blue eyes empty, his dark hair ruffled, his face still, carved. She knew her mother was worried about her, but she couldn't explain. She didn't think her mother would understand. Her father might have done. But he was dead. It was almost a relief when the month was up. She didn't think she could stand any more of her mother's unhappy looks, her sighs, which made her feel doubly guilty.

She rang Sally, ignored all her questions, queries, exclamations, merely told her when she would be back. On the train she gave herself a good talking to. She would make a new life for herself. In a few months she would probably be unable to remember what Marcus looked like. She would find new interests, make new friends. She was still talking to herself as she lugged her suitcase along the platform at King's Cross. It seemed to have acquired extra weight since she had boarded the train in Scotland, and she was forced to rest every few yards before staggering on a bit further. As she reached the barrier, she halted in shock, her suitcase thudding unheeded to her feet. Marcus was standing just the other side—and all her resolutions, her stern talks, dispersed like mist in the breeze. She felt such a wave of love for him wash over her that she closed her eyes in despair. 'No,' she whispered. 'No.'

'You all right, luv?' Only, she didn't hear the ticket collector's concerned question. Didn't hear anything, see anything, except Marcus. Elegant, that was what he was, she thought weakly. Elegant and important-looking, and so impossibly dear. He was wearing a dark three-piece suit, his white shirt-collar crisp, the pale grey tie knotted exactly in place. And she looked like a gypsy, she thought in despair. Why on earth had she worn old blue cotton trousers with matching shirt, the sleeves rolled untidily back? Why hadn't she worn something smart?

His dark hair was ruffled across his forehead, as it had been then, and it seemed to add emphasis to those blue, blue eyes that stared back as though he, too, needed to make a complete inventory. Even from the distance she stood from him, they were as clear and bright as a midsummer sky. But she didn't know if they were empty. As he began to move, in slow motion it seemed, her heart lurched painfully. Then he was in front of her, his face intent, purposeful, and the blue eyes weren't empty, she saw, they were blazing. Electric. Beneath the ticket collector's bemused gaze, he picked her up, moved her to one side and dragged her into his arms, his face finding the warm curve of her neck. And Toby clutched him tight and burst into tears. She cried out all the pent-up misery and hurt, cried for her father, herself, for her loneliness and pain. With her fingers clenched in his immaculate lapels, she uttered broken little phrases, about her selfishness, her stupidity, telling him she was sorry, over and over again, her voice thick and uneven. The argument, the accusations they'd hurled at each other, no longer mattered. Nothing mattered except that he was here.

'Oh, Marcus,' she wept, 'I've been so miserable.' Raising her stained and blotchy face to him, she gave a long, hard sniff. 'I blamed you and everyone else for my inadequacies . . .' Her voice tailed off as she found it hurt to speak and became aware instead that his eyes were dark and almost anguished. His body was rigid with tension and fresh tears washed into her eyes. 'Oh, Marcus!'

'Don't,' he groaned, his warm palms coming up to frame her poor little face, and then he lowered his head to kiss away the tears, his tongue tasting the salt. Yet what began as gentle comfort became too much for both of them, and their mouths sought each other in desperate hunger.

They exchanged kisses that were almost savage in their intensity, a breathless, mindless exercise, so much need and longing in both of them. Sliding his arms round her, he lifted her to his own height, his mouth not leaving hers, then leaned his body hard against her so that she was pressed impossibly tight between him and the metal grating of the barrier. His hard, thrusting body was hurting her, a pain that she needed, welcomed, to make it real. As his mouth ground painfully against hers, she bit into his lip, then soothed it with her tongue, straining to be closer, still closer.

'Oh, God,' he said thickly, his breathing ragged. 'Oh, God, Toby.' And, lowering her gently to her feet, he leaned his head on top of hers, his fingers tangling urgently in the soft strands of hair that had given up the unequal struggle to stay confined.

'Still haven't managed to discipline it, have you?' he breathed huskily.

'No,' she croaked. 'Do you really think that anything that belongs to me would ever be disciplined?' Hugging him tight, her body shaking, she whispered, 'I'm sorry.'

'For what?' he said thickly, wrenching her back to look down into her face. 'For driving me insane? Haunting me? Telling the truth?'

'As I saw it,' she murmured, her eyes locked with his, a weakness flowing through her at the feel of him, the solid strength. 'And for trying to change you, for not understanding, for being stupid—oh, for everything real or imagined,' she murmured, giving a wobbly smile. 'I truly only ever came to work for you because of the rent.'

'Think I even care?' he said throatily. As his eyes moved to her soft, swollen mouth and his fingers dug painfully into her shoulders, Toby leaned her whole length against him and stared up into his face, unable to drag her eyes away.

'Did Sally tell you?' she said, which was a stupid

thing to ask; it could hardly have been chance that had brought him to King's Cross at just that particular moment, and Sally had been the only one who knew what train she'd be on. Which meant he must have been to the flat, or at least spoken to Sally on the phone. Why hadn't Sally told her? 'Did you tell Sally not to tell me you'd called?' she asked.

'Yes,' he murmured, amusement lightening his eyes for a moment. 'Or that I practically haunted the flat in case you should ring.'

'Oh,' she said lamely. Then, as her mind absorbed that, such a wave of jealousy washed over her as she pictured Marcus with the beautiful Sally, that she asked, 'Pretty, isn't she?' twisting the knife in her overwrought emotions.

'Yes, very pretty,' he said gently, giving a tiny smile that just slightly grooved his cheek. 'But not scatty.'

'No. Not scatty,' Toby murmured with a sigh. 'She doesn't tell lies, either,' and was horrified to find herself on the verge of tears again. 'Oh, God!'

'Don't,' he groaned. 'Oh, don't.' And he clutched her so close she thought her ribs might break. But she didn't want him to stop. Didn't want him to ever stop. As he roughly pulled her head back, his mouth sought hers again and she dragged herself up until her body fitted smoothly to his. Her fingers clenched in his hair as she eagerly opened her mouth to his. Only, that wasn't enough, and she pressed feverish kisses to his mouth, his cheeks, anywhere she could reach as he responded with an urgency that was almost violent. She wanted to touch him, feel that warm flesh beneath her palms, and her fingers desperately sought the buttons of his waistcoat and shirt, only to halt uncertainly as he drew in a ragged breath.

'Dear God, Toby,' he muttered thickly. 'Not in the middle of the station.'

'What?' Staring round her in sudden horror, registering the amused glances they were receiving, she blushed scarlet, and hastily refastened the buttons she'd undone. 'I forgot where we were,' she mumbled, embarrassed. Staring at him, at the wicked amusement glinting in his eyes, she gave a shaky grin. 'Won't do much for your image, will it?'

'You think that's all I care about, Toby? My image?'

'I don't know,' she whispered. 'I don't know what you want.'

'All of you,' he said simply, his voice catching. 'I want to keep you safe. I want your dear little face on the pillow beside mine every morning when I wake.'

'Oh, don't!' she choked. 'I don't want to have a dear face.'

'Why?' he asked unevenly, his warm palms coming up to frame it. 'It's a beautiful face. A happy, laughing face. And I need to see it each day of my life!'

'Oh, Marcus,' she sighed, closing her eyes for a moment, almost afraid to hope that he might mean it. 'I'm so unsuitable. You'll get bored with me,' she prophesied. 'We have nothing in common.'

'Yes, we do,' he said almost harshly, dropping a fierce kiss on her mouth.

'What? Backgammon, tennis? Hardly intellectual pursuits. You're a clever man, Marcus!' she said insistently. 'Brilliant, Frank Dawson said. How could you want a scatty little idiot like me? I'll exasperate you, infuriate you . . .'

'Please God,' he said fervently, 'you will also make me human. Show me the beauty in the day. Tease me. Love me.' Then, staring down into her worried face, he added huskily, 'I need you to love me, Toby. I need you to keep me sane.'

'I do love you. I love you so much I don't think I can bear it. But I'm so afraid I'll be inadequate. I don't know very much about business. You know I don't. I won't be able to discuss your day with you when you come home. I mean, look what a mess I made of being a secretary. I thought secretaries just did typing and shorthand, answered the phone, did a bit of filing. It never occurred to me that there were diaries to keep, appointments to be juggled, flights, arrangements, being one step ahead of you all the time . . .'

'Toby, Toby,' he broke in, then as someone staggered against them he turned to glare. Then as if realising how ridiculous he was being, he grinned shippishly, muttering, 'You see how confused you've got me? The most important conversation of our lives and we're holding it in the middle of King's Cross!' Grasping her arm, he began to urge her toward the exit, only to halt as the ticket collector chased after them with Toby's case. Giving the man a wry grin, he virtually pulled Toby outside to where his car was parked.

Putting her into the passenger seat, he walked swiftly round to climb in behind the wheel. Turning to face her, he grasped her hands. 'Now, where was I? Oh, yes.' Pulling her urgently toward him, he kissed her hard, with a thoroughness that melted her bones, then left her bereft as he determinedly set her back into her seat.

'Hello,' he murmured throatily.

'Hello,' she whispered back and, stretching out her hand, touched it gently against his face.

'Talk first,' he said thickly, and, taking a deep breath, returning her hand to her lap, he asked, 'Do you remember when I came into the nursery and you were bathing Peter? I wanted it to be real, Toby! For me! A wife! A child! And I wanted you both! For me. I told you that, didn't I?' And when she nodded dazedly, not sure that he'd told her that at all, he continued firmly, 'That day by the pool, watching you, wanting you. Dear God, Toby, how I wanted you! And I kept thinking, it could be like this. Only when I was alone, in my saner moments, I denied it. It was ludicrous to even consider it. Yet I spent so much time at work just doodling, staring idly into space . . .' Giving a long, shaky sigh, his eyes holding hers, he continued, 'I'm twelve years your senior, Toby— which, said quickly, doesn't sound so much,' he muttered, giving her a boyish grin, 'yet you sometimes made me feel so old, and I'd think back to when I was twenty-four, and it was just an empty place. I couldn't remember being anything other than what I'd become. You kept giving me glimpses of a youth I'd never had.'

Putting her hand up again, needing to touch him, feel his warmth, she rested her palm gently his cheek and he turned his mouth into it, closing his eyes for a moment. 'At university you were young,' she pointed out, 'you said so, playing the guitar and everything.'

But not young like you. Not—carefree. Not ever that. And stop interrupting, or else I'll never say it all—especially when you look at me like that,' he added softly.

'Sorry,' she murmured, not sorry at all. She didn't want him to talk, explain, she wanted to kiss him.

'Stop it,' he muttered thickly. Taking another, longer breath that severely tested the buttons on his waistcoat, he went on, 'That night in the bedroom before Peter woke up, I damned near raped you! I always want you!' he muttered on a broken laugh. 'I have this irresistible urge to take you, in the garden, the pool, in the kitchen—in the car. It's crazy and exciting and terrifying. The women that I've known don't like to be—well, they don't like to be . . .'

'Disarrayed?' she put in a trifle waspishly, snatching her hand back.

'Yes! That describes it exactly,' he grinned, capturing her hand and returning it to his face. 'Disarrayed. They . . .'

'Marcus! I do not want to hear how other women make love to you!'

'No, sorry,' he murmured, giving a throaty laugh. 'I was just trying to explain why I find you so appealing. I had all this worked out, you know. What I was going to say—and now I'm saying it all back to front.' Then, pulling his mouth down ruefully at the corners, he asked, 'Can I just tell you about that night we spent together?' She pulled a little face, but he continued. 'Usually, after the—act, if you like, the woman has turned away, put space between us, and that was it all it was, an act. Yet you curved against me, your breasts against my back, your thigh beneath mine, and I lay awake a long time just thinking about it, enjoying the feel of you. Your warmth, your generosity. As though it had been really enjoyable, that you needed to be close to me.'

'I did,' she said softly. 'I still do. More than anything on this earth, it's what I want. It's just that it seems so inconceivable.'

'Why? I want to come home to a haven of warmth, peace, laughter. I want to learn to relax, enjoy life before it't too late—before I become like my father,' he added, his beautiful eyes darkening fractionally. Then, tracing one finger gently down her cheek, moving the wisps of hair aside, he murmured softly, 'Did you think I wanted an empty-headed beauty who thinks more of the state of her nails than of my feelings? Do you? Do you really think I don't have a heart that can be broken?'

'No,' she whispered.

'I'm impatient, I know. And arrogant. Too many years being deferred to in business, I expect. I know I hurt you, all those terrible things I said, but—oh, Toby, when I found out about the lies—it hurt,' he said simply. 'I didn't know anything could hurt so much. I'd gone to work that morning, a silly smile on my face, and I thought, when I get home, I'll tell her, tell her that I'm falling in love with her, and then in the post was that letter from your old school.'

'I know,' she said gently, caressing his cheek. 'I know.'

'Do you think it's too late for me to change? I lacked trust, I know, but I have this vision, Toby, of a house filled with laughter, children. Is it an impossible vision?'

'With me?' she whispered, hardly daring to believe he meant what he was saying.

'With you,' he confirmed gently.

'But I won't be very suitable,' she said, masochistically needing to point out every pitfall that he might not have thought of. 'You're so beautiful.'

'Beautiful?' he asked, astonished, his eyebrows practically climbing into his hair.

'Yes. You are, you know. Not in an effeminate way or anything, but you are beautiful. You think I don't see other women looking at you? Wanting you? I shall be horribly jealous.'

'You won't have any need, Toby,' he said gently, and with such an expression of love in his eyes that she had to swallow drily. 'You think I don't know what I want?'

'Oh, Marcus, I don't know,' she said confusedly. 'I'm not a bit sophisticated or anything.'

'Why on earth should I want my wife sophisticated?'

'Because people like you always have sophisticated wives. Like Lydia,' she muttered, punishing herself further.

'People like me?' he queried comically. 'We're not back to whips and bondage, are we? And don't, for God's sake, wish Lydia on to me.'

'You loved her once,' she interrupted.

'Did I?' he asked whimsically. 'I wonder. I think it was probably more a sort of infatuation. She was incredibly beautiful. I have this recurring nightmare that she didn't go off to the States with an American millionaire and I ended up marrying her! And just to set the record straight, Lydia did not jilt me. It was the other way round.'

'But everyone said . . .'

'I know. I do have some gentlemanly instincts, Toby. There's not so much stigma attached to a man being jilted.'

'Oh,' she murmured, then gave him a warm, wide smile. 'That was nice of you.' And when he laughed and squeezed her hand, she asked, 'Why did she come back?'

'I believe the American divorced her. I don't know. Don't really care.'

'You wouldn't have got back together?'

'Heavens, no! Despite your opinion to the contrary. Yet if I hadn't met you,' he continued softly, 'I would probably, eventually, have married someone else of tha ilk and never known that some ladies make love with enormous enthusiasm, that they tease and poke fun——'

'But they don't look like the wives of wealthy and successful men! I mean, can you see me at some of these functions you have to attend?' she demanded, having got some idea of the sort of life he must lead from Mrs Henson. 'Can you really imagine me at some posh do? I'd say all the wrong things.'

'Nonsense! You'll liven things up no end. In fact, I quite look forward to letting you loose on all those dull, dried-up old sticks and their awful wives. I predict, Miss Toby Anderson, that you will be an absolute wow. And will you please stop trying to find excuses not to marry me? It's doing my confidence absolutely no good at all. I'd much rather you told me how much you love me, how much you want me,' he said rather huskily. 'And I quite liked that bit about my beauty.'

'Oh, Marcus,' she said with a soft little laugh, 'I do wish you'd be serious.'

'I don't want to be serious. I've spent my whole life being serious! I want to make love to you. Very, very badly. It's been such a long time,' he breathed softly.

'Yes,' she murmured, her insides liquefying. Leaning forward, she lay her face against his chest. 'I didn't know that one man's touch could set me alight. One man's smile would melt my bones.' And, as he went to speak, she looked up and covered his mouth with her hand. 'You said once there was a need to say words that neither of us could say. Well, the need got worse, and I do need to say them, despite my trying to find excuses. It's just that I'd rather lose you now, then later, because I couldn't bear that.'

'Is that why you ran away?' When she nodded, he said raggedly, 'I couldn't believe you'd gone. I came home early . . .' And he sounded so bewildered, so hurt, that she moved to hold him, then tutted crossly at the gear-stick in the way. Moving reluctantly back to her own seat, she whispered, 'I couldn't take any more. I'm such a coward, Marcus. All that emotion frightened me.'

'And now?'

'I discovered that it was far worse without you,' she said simply. 'And now that I know you love me—well, it's different,' she said, sounding surprised. And it was true. Now that she knew she had his love, she thought she could be strong. 'I couldn't understand how my mother could lay herself open to that again. Getting re-married,' she explained when he looked puzzled. 'Only now I do. I thought I could bury it all, push you out of my mind. And I couldn't,' she said helplessly.

'No. No more could I.'

'I do love you, Marcus,' she whispered, and the blue eyes that were so beautiful darkened. They pierced hers. Seemed to see right into her soul. Putting up a shaky hand, she slipped her fingers into the dark, silky hair. Smiling rather mistily at him, she reached across to touch her mouth softly, hesitantly to his. 'Did you ever find out who leaked the merger?'

'No,' he said rather absently. 'Someone talking out of turn, maybe—an overheard conversation, it doesn't matter. Not at the moment. Tell me you love me,' he ordered huskily.

'I love you. I want to keep saying it, I want to touch you and hold you . . .'

'Oh Toby,' he groaned. 'Don't say that when I'm in no position to do anything about it. Unless you want to get us both arrested.'

'Then put us in a position where you can,' she said softly.

Staring at her, holding her eyes, he growled, 'Put your seat-belt on. We'll be driving very fast.'

His hands shaking, he put the car in gear. Never had his flat seemed so far away.

Harlequin Presents.

Coming Next Month

Available in October wherever paperback books are sold, or through Harlequin Reader Service:

In the U.S.
901 Fuhrmann Blvd.
P.O. Box 1397
Buffalo, N.Y. 14240-1397

In Canada
P.O. Box 603
Fort Erie, Ontario
L2A 5X3

Harlequin American Romance®

Gull Cottage

SUMMER.

The sun, the surf, the sand . . .

One relaxing month by the sea was all Zoe, Diana and Gracie ever expected from their four-week stays at Gull Cottage, the luxurious East Hampton mansion. They never thought they'd soon be sharing those long summer days—or hot summer nights—with a special man. They never thought that what they found at the beach would change their lives forever. But as Boris, Gull Cottage's resident mynah bird said: "Beware of summer romances. . . ."

Join Zoe, Diana and Gracie for the summer of their lives. Don't miss the GULL COTTAGE trilogy in American Romance: #301 *Charmed Circle* by Robin Francis (July 1989), #305 *Mother Knows Best* by Barbara Bretton (August 1989) and #309 *Saving Grace* by Anne McAllister (September 1989).

GULL COTTAGE—because a month can be the start of forever . . .

Have You Ever Wondered If You Could Write A Harlequin Novel?

Here's great news—Harlequin is offering a series of cassette tapes to help you do just that. Written by Harlequin editors, these tapes give practical advice on how to make your characters—and your story—come alive. There's a tape for each contemporary romance series Harlequin publishes.

Mail order only

All sales final
